RAVEN KING

SPARROW MAN

BOOK FOUR

M. R. PRITCHARD

Paperback ISBN: 978-1-957709-33-8

Dumb Ways to Die

Have you ever tried to fly? Takeoff is a bitch. Sparrow made it look easy—heck seagulls make it look easy. Nothing prepares you for the lack of strength in your back, the choking feeling in your throat, the uselessness of your legs, the feeling of purely sucking at life.

"Go!" Skeele shouts. "Launch yourself. Jump! Like this." He catapults himself into the air; his wings whip out and then he's heading toward the Hellsky. Effortless. Like a damned eagle on the coast. Of course, he's big and muscular and has had a lot of time to perfect flying. I flex my bicep and the smallest muscle bulges. Maybe I should do some push-ups. Skeele lands nearby, the dust of Hell swirling around his boots as he stomps down. "Now," he motions with the swoop of his arm, "it's your turn."

"I'm tired." I cross my arms and tip my head, trying to loosen tense neck muscles.

"You've been sleeping all day." He steps closer. "You shouldn't be tired. You sleep more than a baby." He keeps stepping closer.

Skeele is one big son-of-a-bitch and there was one point in time that he terrified the fuck out of me, but not anymore. He doesn't scare the ruler of Hell. I went through too much to fear anyone anymore, even this giant Hellion with horns and sharp teeth.

"Do it, Meg." He's too close. "Fly!" he roars. I jump and take two steps away. "What are you afraid of?" he asks.

I hold out my arms, directing him to stay away. "I just need some space."

"Don't be afraid of failing. None of us came out of the womb with wings. We all had to learn." He's so calm and encouraging, not like the Hellions of the past. He's not like the ones who would rather kill first and ask questions later. Sparrow taught him better.

"I've already failed enough." I roll my shoulders, loosening my back muscles. There's nothing there. It doesn't even feel like anything is thinking of being there. No wings. Nothing.

"Why?" Skeele scoffs. "Because you lost Sparrow?"

"Shut up." I glare at him.

He moves closer. "You're just hangry." Skeele frowns. "I could help you."

I have eaten nearly every Twinkie in Hell, every bag of chips, every orange soda, everything that might send a middle-aged man on a quick trip to cardiac arrest. Nothing will fill my stomach like a little bit of fresh blood would. Like a little sip of Sparrow's blood. But Skeele's blood. No thanks. Not on my life would I drink from him. That's crossing the line. Fresh blood brings the lust. I'm saving that for one man in my life.

Skeele's holding out his forearm, the blood pulsing through his thick veins. I can hear it; *whoosh-whoosh-whoosh* thundering in my ears. My mouth fills with saliva, anticipating the sweet flush of fresh blood. My eyes flick to his face. He's not Sparrow. Not even close. There are no green eyes, no mussed brown hair, no tick of insanity.

"Fucker," I mutter as I stomp away.

"It's not going to go away," Skeele shouts in my direction. "The hunger will never go away. If you don't do something about it, you're going to do something you regret."

Overgrown grass sweeps my legs as I walk to the nearby Jeep Wrangler. I didn't want to practice near the castle, didn't want the others to see that a loser who couldn't fly ruled them. They quivered in the presence of my grandfather. They must do the same for me.

A Northern Flicker whistles a trill from the hood of the Jeep. I stop. These birds keep haunting me. With Sparrow and the others around it was kinda endearing, now every flutter is a sign, every chirp a warning.

"They'll never grow out your back if you don't try," Skeele shouts from the field behind me. "They need an urge to sprout!"

I pick up a rock and throw it at the hood of the Jeep, scaring away the songbird. I gotta get out of here. I need to shake this feeling of defeat.

The thud of heavy footsteps is suddenly behind me. Large hands grip the waistband of my leather pants and under my arm.

"What the—" I kick, trying to escape but my feet are lifted off the ground.

The fucker doesn't know when to stop. "They'll never appear unless you try," he grumbles in my ear as he tosses me in the air.

My stomach remains on land as I pedal my arms and legs as my eyes scan the treetops.

"No!" I shout as gravity pulls me down.

Skeele is in the air; he grabs the back of my pants again and tosses me higher. "Fly!" he shouts.

My stomach flops like that day Noah and me skipped our exams, stole a car, and spent the day at Seabreeze. We rode the Jack Rabbit so many times I puked. I'm ready to puke again. Each time I fall, Skeele tosses me higher and it gets harder and harder to breathe. The air is thin this high up in Hellsky.

He lets me fall over and over again.

"You piece of shit!" I swallow back bile. "I will throw you in the pit for this," I shout.

It's hard to stop your arms and legs from churning in the air. I don't have time to reach maximum velocity like in that movie. I twist, my back facing the ground, and flip him off.

He's coming at me from above, just far enough away to induce panic. He laughs after glancing at my hands. I wonder for a split second if this is how my grandfather felt as his body fell to the ground. He was gone though. I'd sucked every drop of life out of him.

Skeele grabs me just before I hit the ground. He settles me on my feet and his wings fold against his back.

Fired up, I grab my blade, kick him in the shin, and drop him to kneeling. I slam my foot into the center of his chest and kick him back. Standing on his chest, I set the tip of my blade under his chin.

"I could kill you for that." I swallow down the thickness in my throat. I move the tip of the blade to his chest and press harder, until it pierces the first layer of his gear. "I still might kill you for that."

He shrugs thick shoulders. "I'm just trying to help." He twists his neck to the side, just ever so slightly, so I can see the pulse of his jugular.

Whoosh-whoosh-whoosh. It's hypnotic. I find myself leaning closer, tempted. The closer I get, the more I can smell him. It's not bad. Not repulsive. He's clean. Different than the Hellions of my past. I involuntarily lick my lips.

He smiles.

"I fucking hate Hellions," I remind Skeele before I stand up straight and step off his chest. I walk away, around the Jeep and toward the empty, crumbling road.

"Don't you want a ride back to the castle?" he shouts from the ground.

"Go fuck yourself." I wave with my middle fingers.

"Don't run away, Meg," Skeele grumbles.

But I'm good at running. It's really the only thing I've ever been good at. The only thing that's ever really saved me. Why not run away? Running away sounds like fun right now. I could ignore all my duties. No longer have this weight of being inept on my shoulders. Running away could be just what I need. Running away could be the best thing ever.

The walk back to the castle isn't long. I could *poof* and be there in an instant, but I need to walk off what just happened. I've got to burn that energy. I've traveled the trail more than a few times after a failed flying lesson. The only worries are the dead, schlepping it along and moaning like cows. They stay away from me now that I have a real title down here. It took me a long time not to run when I see them. Still, their shadows and moaning make me uneasy.

I take a deep breath and remind myself of who I am. "My name is Meg Clark. I killed my mother the day I was born. My father is the Archangel Gabriel. My grandfather was Lucifer, until I killed him. I've done some very bad things. I even own a blade that was forged in the fires of Hell. Oh, and I slid my blade into my boyfriend's heart releasing his last bit of grace and now he's lost to me." Can't forget that last bit. Icing on the fruitcake of shit-fuckery.

It sounds so impressive and depressing. But what I wouldn't give to escape to a beach or a bar and drown my sorrows in sunlight and liquor. But I can't escape to the Earthen plane. Or at least I haven't figured out how to—yet—without getting caught.

The smell of woodsmoke and pine gets stronger the closer I get to the castle nestled in the burning caves. I step foot inside. Creatures scurry to the shadows and still as I walk by. It's a far cry from my little white house with picket fence in Gouverneur. That was a life I was never meant to live, Sparrow once told me. How different my life has become now. I wouldn't say I've fully embraced taking Lucifer's place, but I'm getting there.

There is someone missing here. A large, lurking Angel turned

Hellion known as Sparrow. He is mine and I am his, and I must figure out where the heck he went. I tap my fingers over the tattoo on my chest, a watercolor of a sparrow in flight, wishing it would bring him back to me. I whistle a light trill in remembrance. I miss my monster something terrible. He is the only one who has ever shown me love and caring and truth. He may be a monster, but he's mine. Most days, I'm pretty sure that I'm the bigger monster.

My stomach growls. The bloodlust doesn't want to wait for him. I can't cure it. There's only remission and relapse. Fuck it all. I make my way to the kitchen, my footsteps angry and hollow on ages old stone floors. The kitchen staff hear me coming. They run, which is good. I'm losing all control just like Skeele warned. The pressure builds as I near the door and slam it open, then slam it closed. My stomach growls so loud I'm sure all of Hell hears it. Nothing is sacred in this kitchen, in this moment. There's cake in the fridge, decadent and sugar filled. Someone spent hours decorating it with black roses made of buttercream. I dip my hand into it, grab a giant piece, and shove it in my mouth. I open a container of milk and pour it down my throat. This continues. Cheese, pepperoni, steak, chicken soup, ancient wines and spirits, sugar-baked carrots and loaded fries, chips, dips, Twinkies, and Hostess cakes. Everything I've asked the staff of the castle to stock for me, I tear through it all in record time. I pause, only to look around the kitchen and see my work. The place is wrecked, and my stomach is so full I might vomit. I slump to the floor, my back against the fridge that's covered in sugary fingerprints and splatters of food. I slide to the side and lay on my back, my stomach bloated, my throat bursting. I should weigh five-hundred pounds with the things I've eaten down here trying to fill the void. I just want one thing. One thing would stop this hunger. Biting into Sparrow's neck. And if we were both naked, that would help. That would fill another need.

I close my eyes in disgust and focus on the feeling of the cold, stone floor under my head. There was a time when my cupboards were empty. When I was more often hungry than full. I wrestled a dog for a peanut butter and jelly and won. That was a highlight in my life in childhood. Some would cry at the memory. It wasn't worse than trading my freedom to live with Jim for all those months. At least my stomach is full of food, my womb is empty, and I've got a handful of Hellions who will protect me until the end. Things aren't all bad. My life is kinda like those posters in elementary school of the kitten hanging on a branch. I've just got to hang on there until I can figure all this out.

"You know, you're kind of a slob." Noah looks down at me.

"If I say 'I couldn't help myself' would it matter?" I ask. The bloodlust is calmer but still there, threatening to explode under my skin. Noah can't help me. He's a ghost. A soul of the Astral plane and tied to me. Still, he's the best friend a girl could ever have.

"You are the ruler of this place, so I guess you can do whatever you want." Noah shrugs.

"Why does it have to be like this?" I ask.

"How would you like it to be, Meg? Or should I call you Lucifer?"

"Never call me that." I glare at him.

Noah spins on one foot, stomps down with his legs straddling my knees, and reaches for my hands. "Come on. You look pathetic. Get up."

I nod and sniff away the tears threatening the corners of my eyes. "Why are you always so nice to me?" I ask.

Noah smiles and everything is better. You'd know if you'd ever seen Noah or Jack smile, handsome isn't enough to describe it. "I got you into plenty of trouble when I was alive. I guess this is my penance." He pulls me to my feet. "Gosh, Meg, you look like crap." He looks me up and down. "And those leathers are looking a little tight on your ass. Since you've already scared the kitchen staff to death, how about you go clean yourself up and I'll take care of this."

I nod and rub my face with filthy, food covered hands.

"Go." Noah prods my rib, pushing me away.

"Do not tell anyone about this," I threaten as I walk away.

"Wouldn't think of it."

I head to my room, down long hallways and rooms I have yet to explore. I should probably learn what lies within my own castle, but I don't have the mindset for it today. I close the heavy wooden door to my room and move a chair in front of the door handle. There's a Northern Flicker on my balcony, could be the same one from my flying lesson. I whistle but it's nothing like the wonderful way the others do it. I blame my sucking at whistling on the sugar and salt swelling my tongue and make my way to the bathroom. I start the shower and turn the handle until it's nice and hot. Hot enough to melt off my shame and the sugar crusted under my fingernails. Maybe if I melt off the top layer of my skin those wings will show up. I unstrap my blade and set it on the counter before stripping down. I don't bother to look at the tattoos and scars before I get in the blasting water. Maybe another day; I don't want to remember all of that right now. I wash and then stand in the stream of water and let it massage my neck and shoulders. Closing my eyes, I remember Sparrow touching my neck, the sides of my waist. The deep ebb of his voice, the roughness of his fingertips, the swipe of his shaggy brown hair against my skin. I shiver and slam my hand over the knob, turning the water off. Damn it. I wrap myself in a towel and step out onto a plush bathmat. I should be grateful for all I have down here. I didn't grow up with fluffy bath towels and bathmats. My feet didn't dry instantly as they hit a plush terrycloth mat. No, all I had for a long, long time was a single, threadbare towel that got washed when I remembered and barely soaked up the water on my skin, let alone the floor. The amount of time I've been on the plane of Hell can't erase the memory of bathwater airdrying off my skin and causing a chill in the dead of winter, bone deep. That could be why I turn the water so hot: it's a memory chilled in my bones that I can't warm.

As I brush my teeth, I swipe my hand across the mirror. My

hair is too long, brushing my shoulders. I can't stand it. I search the bathroom drawers until I find a pair of scissors and go to town. Snip, snip, snip, until my hair is a chin-length bob, just like I like it. I stare at my reflection. I count to ten before I cut bangs. Bangs cure a lot. Plenty of women going through a personal crisis get bangs. I shake the short pieces loose. Bangs will do just fine right now.

I clean up the pieces of my black hair in the sink and throw them in the trash. The mess I left in the kitchen was bad enough. I need a little redemption in this place. I guess I'll start by not making Noah clean up my mess in the bathroom.

I make my way to the closet, open the door, and flick the light on. There are rows of clothes that Clea gave me; leather pants and skimpy tops, jackets and flimsy undergarments, stuff I could have never afforded on the Earthen plane. Couldn't get this stuff at Wal-Mart. Heck, I'd have to go to the mall four hours away from home. I chose dark jeans, a bright blue T-shirt, a leather jacket, matching black undergarments, and a pair of sturdy boots. Always dress for travel and ready to flee, that's one thing life has taught me. Be ready to run. Be ready to fight and then run. I get dressed in the closet and when I step out, Noah's back.

"Funny, you don't look like you gorged in full fat-ass mode." His eyes scan me head to toe. "Bangs?"

I shrug. "Better than some things I could have done."

"They look good." He sits at the table near the balcony and tosses seeds onto the railing, making a game of it as some bounce and fall to the yard below.

I sit next to him. We watch the songbirds fly from treetop to railing and back again. There's not as many as when Sparrow and Nightingale were here. Those days the railing was lined with colorful birds.

"I guess I should bring some seeds," Noah says as he stands. "What do you want me to get you?" Noah asks.

"A vial of Sparrow's blood so I can stop this craving." I settle my hands over my stomach.

Noah laughs and whistles a gloomy trill. "You'll have to go get that yourself."

"How about fried chicken and buttermilk biscuits?" I ask.

"You want something to drink? Or are you going to choke those down dry so you can remember what it's like to have Sparrow wrapping his hands round your neck?"

"Go fuck yourself, Noah." I wouldn't be so mad if he weren't the least bit right.

"Would if I could. Actually, it's all I have left to do now that someone married off my girlfriend to my brother. And now he gets to raise my child." He glares at me.

"Sorry 'bout that." It was a pretty shitty thing that happened. But the fate of the world was at stake. I don't apologize further, instead I say, "I'd like an orange Crush Big Gulp. No ice."

"Fine." He disappears to go wherever he goes to get me food.

I stare out into Hellsky and contemplate what the heck I need to do first. I don't get far with my thoughts before there's a knock on my door. Well, more of a slamming fist pounding relentlessly like the cops on a hot lead.

"Go away," I shout.

"Open the door," Skeele's rough voice says.

"Nope."

He tries the handle. "Meg. Open the door."

I close my eyes. "I never get a moment of goddamned peace in this place."

"You spend plenty of time having a pity party in your room." The door rumbles again. "Open the door."

"Open it yourself."

Wood creaks and snaps. The chair I had propped against the door goes flying across the room with splinters of aged wood. "Your wish is my command." Skeele bows and steps into my room.

I grip the blade that's strapped to my thigh. "I'm not a fan of Hellions who act like that."

Skeele crosses the room and drops himself into a leather club chair near the far wall. "Look, I came to apologize. I shouldn't have thrown you."

"Ya think?"

"I'm just trying to help." He crosses his legs, an ankle resting on his knee. "You need to learn to fly. It will help you travel faster, and it could save you one day." He pauses. "It just, it took you a very long time to recover from your fall. I sat here for months watching you."

"Thanks for that," I mutter.

Skeele drops his foot and leans forward. "No, Meg, I don't think you understand. Hell was unruled for months while you were out of it. And now you won't commit. The Hellion leader is MIA. Souls are dropping into Hell at record pace." He rubs his bald, horned head. "The Safe Houses and Deacons are overrun."

"Good. I haven't forgotten what they did to me. They're lucky I don't strike every one of them down." My fingers smooth over the blade strapped to my thigh as I imagine chopping their heads off. I'd love to kill a Deacon or a hundred of them, but they are one of those strange beings that help organize the realms. I can't kill them. I just have to stand back and watch them meddle.

"Then who would greet your new souls?" Skeele asks. "Who would collect the sins of the dead and offer their last chance to repent? There is organization down here, whether you understand it or not. Whether you like it or not. The dead need to learn their place, they still have a life after death. Would you like them to wake like you did when you were in that coma and oscillating between realms without knowing it? You were lucky to find Sparrow right away. Can't you at least hope for better for the ones you rule over?"

I stare him down. The fuck. Hitting me in the feels.

"I know you're bad, Meg," Skeele keeps talking. "Bad to the

bone like Sparrow always said. But you have an ounce of compassion for these souls. I know it. Stop playing tough."

I move my hand off the blade and cross my arms. "I might. But it doesn't help me dislike the Deacons any less."

"They've learned their place. You won." He throws up his hands. "You literally sucked the life out of Lucifer mid-air for all of Hell to see."

"I did do that." I nod.

There is a moment of silence as I contemplate the future. I can't go on without Sparrow. The way it's going these days we've spent more time apart than together. He's spent more time trapped in the abject recesses of his mind than remembering who I am and who we are together.

"What are you going to do?" Skeele asks.

"Find Sparrow."

Skeele smirks, showing sharp teeth. "Excellent. It's about time you move forward on that."

I'm gonna try to move on but I won't forget my grandfather, Lucifer's, last warning. "An Archangel who's lost all of his grace now tattooed tailbone to scalp, unrecognizable to many. He's out there on the Earthen plane, collecting souls for *me*." Not anymore. He's collecting souls for me. Hell is my realm. I am Lucifer. But I prefer to be called Meg.

Wayward Son

Sparrow

Dark looked good on Sparrow. So good it didn't even scare away the people of the Earthen plane when they saw him coming. *If* they saw him coming. Without his grace, he didn't need shadows to hide; he is a shadow. Six and a half feet tall and Ireland-grass green eyes turned smokey hazel, the walking dead kept their distance and a few thought that meant he was safe.

Sparrow walked down Redwood Highway headed north. The crashing of Pacific waves on sharp rock quieted his mind and muffled the sound of shuffling feet that were following him from a mile back. Stars sparkled from high above, ready to give their last light before the sun rose.

He'd be in Crescent City soon. Not that Crescent City was a special place, it was just one more town on a long path he'd been walking for months and months; a path without a purpose. Sparrow walked, and killed, and did whatever he wanted.

Sparrow paused, hearing hushed voices. There were signs for DeMartin Campsite. He turned and entered the forest. Boots crunched over sticks and dry pine needles. Sparrow weaved between the redwoods and Douglas-fir. He could smell fire. He could hear the pulsations of twenty carotid arteries filled with blood. Sparrow's mouth watered and his stomach pinched. He slowed, stepped lighter, became a thing of the forest in the night. Invisible. Threatening. A raptor perched ready to attack.

Sparrow lowered to a crouch. There were two men sitting in folding chairs by the fire, shotguns set across their laps. Firelight reflected off a dozen or so tents. Sparrow's mouth watered. One of the men stood and went to relieve himself in the high ferns. Sparrow shifted his weight to drop a knee. A stick broke under him sounding like a firecracker. The other man stood and pointed his shotgun. The second man came back, zipping his pants and gripping his weapon.

"What did you hear?" one asked.

"Stick broke," the other replied.

They moved closer.

Sparrow crouched lower; a panther ready to pounce. There were a few hundred feet between them but the men would have to come into the forest to find him.

"Morning is coming," the one said. "It could be an animal."

"I can't see anything," the other replied.

They moved closer, both hesitating.

Sparrow focused on their throats. The blood was pumping at a fast rate. They were scared. He licked his lips. It had been a long time since he'd had fresh blood. It had been—he stopped thinking, didn't want to remember how good it felt to let go and release the monster inside him.

The men went back to their seats, both keeping a close eye on the shadows in front of them. The fire crackled and drowned out the small sounds of Sparrow shifting his weight. He waited and watched until the sun breached the horizon, and the forest woke.

A woodpecker knocked high in the trees. Sparrow turned to find the bird and observed as it pecked at insects before hopping off to drill another hole. Sparrow enjoyed the noise; it wasn't the usual chirp or chatter but a hollowed knock like bones on a solid door. The noise was comforting, it sounded like home.

The bird flew off, away from the camp toward the thick cropping of trees near the road. Sparrow followed until he stood at the base of a giant redwood, focused on the bird, a tugging deep in his chest. Memories he couldn't pull forth lingered in the back of his mind. It was agitating. The woodpecker knocked a handful of times on the trunk before flitting off. A small black and white striped feather drifted down from the branches.

Sparrow caught it between two fingers, agitation gone.

"It's a pileated woodpecker, you weirdo."

Sparrow turned to find a woman watching him from a few feet away. Her blowtorch-blue hair was a startling contrast to the shadows of the forest and the rising fog. She held a small baseball bat in one hand, her other resting on a handgun secured at her hip. Tattoos twisted up her forearms.

Sparrow tucked the feather in his pocket and moved on, unimpressed.

He didn't bother to be quiet as he walked out of the forest. Twigs crunched under his big boots as he broke the tree line and headed north. He never looked back to see if anyone was following him. He didn't care. He'd eat them if he had to. Heck, he'd eat them if he *wanted* to.

SWEET DREAMS

MEG

It is all happening so fast: traveling between realms, being hunted in that tiny church, Basilica of St. Mary Star of the Sea in Key West, stabbing Sparrow, and taking the last bit of his grace. I will never forget the look on his face, the way his leathery Hellion wings rise to cover him, the speck of light that rises into the clear tropical night.

"They warned me that you'd break my heart. I should've seen it coming when the roses died." Sparrow said those words as I slid the sharp end of my blade past his breastbone and into his heart. I watched in horror as a tiny spec of light escaped his right cocoon of wings and smoldered to nothing. It was a trick, the Scarecrow, Reuben, tricked me. He told me I had to do it to reset the balance.

Everything moves in fast-forward. The Scarecrow made me do it, said Sparrow's grace was disrupting the fiber between Hell and the

Earthen plane. He was wrong. I upset the balance and let a monster loose on the Earthen plane.

I sit up in bed, grip my sweating head, and scream. I can't control it. I rock, silk sheets sticking to my sweating body. What have I done?

The room cools and a wavering figure appears. "Hush, child," Clea sits on the end of my bed. "It's not all doom and torment." Her chilled fingers touch mine. I pull away. "You killed the basilisk and freed me." She shivers. "I'll never be banished to that thing's gut again."

My answer is silence for the first time in my life. Jim would be so proud if he were here to see it. He could never get me to shut up. My mother and I seem to have a curse of our own. Dangerous men and even more dangerous situations. What would one expect from the daughter of Lucifer and a forbidden child.

"If you're feeling badly about the basilisk, you can get another one. You'd just have to hunt it." Clea inspects her fingernails. "They do come in handy, sometimes."

"I'm not sure what I'd need a basilisk for." I throw myself back onto the pillows and pull the damp sheets up to my chin.

While Sparrow was always the one to marinate in shame, now it is my turn. We were supposed to be invincible together. I've ruined that, much like I ruin most things. Still, cutting off Reuben's head felt pretty damn good, the bastard. Ripping open the basilisk's gut to free Clea felt pretty damn good too. And don't get me started on how good draining my grandfather of his blood felt because I'd tell you in a heartbeat that it was better than draining Remiel.

I scoot to the edge of the bed and set my feet on the floor. "I need to get out of here."

Clea rises and moves to the balcony. "Where would you like to go?"

"I need to find Sparrow." I toss the blankets aside and head for the bathroom. I wash my face and brush my teeth, then I head to the closet to find clothes for the day. Through it all, I try to still my mind. I try to focus on my tasks.

Clea is still sitting at the balcony table, Noah sits with her. I sense the presence of Skeele sitting behind me. "I guess it's a party then?"

I glance at the door. It was fixed after Skeele broke it to pieces the other day, but it seems it still does not work at keeping extra people out of my room.

Skeele folds his newspaper and sets it in the chair next to him. "Going somewhere?"

"Yes. I'm going to find Sparrow," I say.

"That's great and all," Skeele says, "but you can't leave."

"What?" I ask.

"You can't leave your realm for the Earthen one. That is God's land." Skeele drops his chin and stares at me. "We have to find another way."

"Oh no. No." I tighten the leather strap of the blade on my thigh. "I'm going. Now." I close my eyes to *poof* the heck out of here, but I don't go anywhere.

"It won't work," Clea warns me.

My eyes flash open. "Why?"

"You took Lucifer's place. You can't go to the Earthen plane on a whim. It's not like before. You must wait for the right time," Clea says.

"This is bullshit," I growl.

Noah smirks, waiting for my temper to come out full blast.

Skeele stands. "It might be. But, there are other things we can do." He motions for me to follow him.

I don't miss the worried look of Clea as I leave the room.

"Where are we going?" I ask.

"The lair," Skeele warns. "The Hellions have a plan."

"Fine." I grip my blade tight. "But no funny business."

"Wouldn't think of it," Skeele promises.

"Toodaloo," Noah says with a wave as I head toward the door.

Skeele leads me down the hall with ages old handspun rugs and down the wide rock stairway. We turn away from the kitchen and head to the lair. My stomach grumbles.

"We have blood," Skeele says.

"It's not the same." I press my hand over my stomach to make it stop.

"It's neutral and will stop you from doing something unexpected. You must be at the top of your game now, Meg."

"I'm always at the top of my game," I lie.

"Uh huh." He mocks and slides a hand down my neck and across my shoulder blade.

"Don't touch me." I shove him as hard as I can. He barely moves.

"I didn't feel any wings. And you're strung tighter than a yo-yo. You're not at the top of your game." Skeele's expression is placid.

There's music blaring from behind the carved door of the lair. A moment of panic passes through me–it always does at this threshold. Bad things happened in here. Next level bullshit went on. I push away the memories of my former fiancée, Jim, stringing me up and stabbing me in the chest. He was the reason I hated the Hellions. I remind myself. I also remind myself that he's dead now. I don't have to worry about Jim or his group of Hellions any longer. Trepidation still lingers though. Hellions are terrible creatures who take on the traits of their leader. The only thing keeping me safe is the fact that Sparrow is still their leader. Skeele is second in command, first now that Sparrow's gone. If this crew falls in line, I don't have a thing to worry about.

Skeele pauses with the door just cracked open. "They know you hate them. They're different than before. Sparrow retrained all of them. He replaced everyone. We have rules now."

I nod. Good ol' Sparrow. My worst fears came true the

moment he became a Hellion to escape his family's curse of turning crazy. My Sparrow. An Archangel turned Hellion.

I straighten my back. "It's fine." I reach past Skeele's arm and push the door open further. The music inside stops and the Hellion's stand as I enter. It's strange, how the memories of before and the reality of now contrast.

"Sit." I wave at them.

"Meg, this is Tukka," Skeele points to a huge Hellion with skin as dark red as a kidney bean. "This is Chel." Chel waves from the shadowed corner of the couch. "And this is Klaus." The last one has a long white beard and white horns on the side of his head.

"Aren't there more?" I ask.

"Yes, they're out," Skeele replies. "They'll be back in a few days once they're done with checking the Safe Houses."

I take this time to try my hand at being the actual leader of Hell. "How's that going?"

Chel speaks first. "There's too many souls arriving daily."

"Too many people dying on the Earthen plane," Skeele clarifies. "But not all of them are arriving here. Some are getting lost."

"They're stuck on the Earthen plane," Chel says.

"There are walking dead there?" I ask.

Skeele nods.

"The demons don't want to stay in line," Klaus says with the cracking of his knuckles. "They want Lucifer."

"Well. I killed him," I reply.

"We are getting that point across, slowly," Klaus says.

Skeele moves across the room and picks up a handful of darts. He starts tossing them at a dart board as we're talking, motioning for the rest of us to join. The others let me go first. Skeele drops five darts in my palm as they tell me about the lesser demons they've had to take care of.

"The one thing to celebrate is that Hell grows stronger with each soul," Skeele says. "You've got to be stronger than your father by now. Damn near stronger than those dicks roaming around the Seven Kingdoms of Heaven."

I shrug. "I don't feel any stronger."

There's a beat of silence.

"Making the demons behave has been a big undertaking," Klaus says as he sends a dart toward the board and hits the center circle.

Tukka shoots next, and his darts hit just off center. He walks forward to pull them out of the board then hands them to me as he walks by.

I haven't played darts in a long time. Not since high school or maybe a little later when I should've been in college. I step up, steady a dart between my fingers. Skeele is talking loudly to Klaus. I throw. The dart hits off to the side of the board. Outside of the circles.

"Boo," Skeele howls.

I get ready to toss the next one. "Didn't know this was a sporting event." I toss the dart, it hits inside the outermost circle.

Someone claps.

"Come on," I sigh. "This is pathetic."

"You can do it," Klaus claps louder.

I toss another dart, and another. They get closer to bullseye each time. I have the final dart pinched between my fingers.

"If she gets this one, first round is on Tukka!" Klaus laughs and slaps Tukka hard on the back.

"And if I miss?" I ask.

There is a pause. "First round is still on Tukka!" Chel shouts. The Hellions bust out in deep laughter.

I smile and toss the dart. It hits the bullseye.

We play five more rounds and I lose every single one. Skeele, Chel, and Klaus prod Tukka.

When the game is over, Klaus says, "Sparrow would be proud."

My shoulders tense.

"That you're here," Skeele clarifies.

I nod as the Hellions lead me to the bar. I sit at the last leather stool at the end of the slab of aged wood. Tukka crouches down and opens the dented refrigerator. When he stands, he has five bags of blood in his hand. Playing bartender, he cuts the bags and pours the blood into glasses. He slides the glasses down to Skeele, Chel, and Klaus. He saves one for himself and sets the last one on the bar top just out of my reach.

I hold my breath, try not to breath in the scent. The others drink, their swallows loud and gulping. I close my eyes for a moment and open them just in time to see Tukka exhale, take the glass away from his mouth, and flash red tinted fangs. He slams his glass down, sending a few drops of blood splattering onto my arm.

The tiny hair on the back of my neck rise. I close my eyes, cross my legs, my back arches, and there's an ache low in my stomach.

Someone growls. It's an animalistic sound but as I try to control myself, I can't discern if it's the Hellion's hunger, a warning, or something else.

My eyes flash open. Uh oh. I scramble down from my seat and run for the door.

The Hellions watch, muscles twitching, never moving.

"I gotta go, boys." I swing the door open with force and slam it closed.

In the hallway, I press my back to the wall and slide down to sitting. My blood splattered arm resting on my knees, I stare at the drops. My stomach growls. I lick the blood drops off.

The low rumble of the Hellions' voices fills the lair.

They're talking about me. They must be. The way I just ran out of there was pathetic. I should have controlled myself. I should have asked for a Shirley Temple and filled my gut with sugar and maybe a few beers. I should have, but I didn't.

I sit on the cold, hard floor until my ass goes numb. No one disturbs me and the Hellion lair goes quiet.

I get back to my room with the sunrise.

"It's not like you to stay out all night with the Hellions." Noah is looking unimpressed as he scans me from head to toe. "Ho."

"Shut up." I throw my jacket at him.

"Is this ... blood?" He inhales with an exaggerated shocked expression. "I hope it's not fresh blood. I'll have to tell Sparrow you've been cheating on him."

"I said shut up." I pull off my shirt and kick off my boots as I walk to the bathroom.

"I'd leave some money on the nightstand but since you rule down here now, I guess it's not necessary." Noah's smiling wide, really loving teasing me.

"Why don't you make yourself useful and go get me some spaghetti and meatballs."

"Heavy on the balls, huh?"

I grab a boot off the floor and throw it at him.

Noah laughs loud before disappearing.

"Asshole," I mutter to myself as I turn on the shower.

There's spaghetti waiting on the table near the balcony. I glance at it, then the bed.

Noah tsks. "I went through a lot to get you that."

"I went through a lot to get you here," I reply.

"We don't need to get so serious." Noah holds up his hands. "I just saw you contemplating sleeping over eating and that's not the Meg I've grown to love. Are you sick?"

"No."

"Sad?"

"Maybe."

"What did those Hellions say to you?" He stands like he's going to go to the lair and set them straight. Good ol' Noah.

"Nothing." I rub my eyes. "They were fine. Spending time with them just made me uneasy," I confess.

"Oh?" he asks. I don't want to explain the blood and the urges.

"Do you think we'll find Sparrow?" I change the subject.

"I don't think *we'll* find him." Noah clasps his hands together. "*You* will find him. You always do, Meg. You'll find him when the time is right. Just like you found me and you found Jack and you found Nightingale. You're good at finding people."

I shrug and head for the bed.

"Oh no. Get over here and choke this spaghetti down. I don't care if you rule down here. Noah doesn't get hot spaghetti dinner from VFW post 5885 for it to rot and grow maggots."

"I'll explode if I eat that now."

"I saw that happen in a Monty Python movie once. Can't wait to see it happen to you." He laughs as I sit and eat. "I didn't bring mints. You'll be fine."

"You're lucky I like you," I say between bites.

"Next time you're going to party in the lair all night, feel free to invite me. Not many parties going on in the Astral realm. Nightingale's been too busy lately to meet me."

"Sure," I say.

I dream of my old house. White fence, green roof. My eyes snap open in the master bedroom. I am reminded of leaks I couldn't afford to fix, a roof threatening to tear off during storm bursts, paint bubbling during the winter thaw when the ice on the roof backed up with melted water. I will be forever stuck in this place. Forever remembering when I'd rather not. Panic sets in. The urge to be elsewhere takes over. I am not meant to be in this place. I run down the stairs and touch the heavy brass doorknob to the front door. It's cool on my fingertips. He'll be home soon. I rip open the door and step onto the entryway. My footsteps sound all the familiar creaks and groans from hundreds of years old wood underneath. My heart beats faster. Panic rises. I'm supposed to be somewhere else. I know it. This can only be one person's doing. I push the screen door open, run across the front porch and down the steps, the solid concrete of the sidewalk pressing into the soles of my feet. I look up at the midnight sky, the full moon, the feathers floating on the wind.

"Night!" I shout into the darkness.

My eyes flash open.

Nightingale is here. Thrush in her arms, she purses her lips and delivers a cheerful trill. "He'd like to see his father." She motions to the baby.

"Jack isn't here," I say. "He can't be here."

"Noah." Her eyes turn dark.

"I really hate it when you control my dreams." I change the subject.

"It was better than what you were dreaming of before." She made a face. "I saved you from that. Would you rather be hating on that old house or hot-ass cell in Heaven?"

At least she chose the lesser of two evils. "Thanks," I say.

Noah materializes. "Nightingale?" He glances at the baby. "What's wrong?"

"We need to talk." Nightingale looks at me and then the open balcony door.

"Be my guest," I motion to the door. "But I'm going back to sleep." I flop back and pull the blanket over my head. My pillow is damp with sweat. As I flip it over, I hear the murmurings of Night and Noah as they talk on the balcony. They're interrupted by the soft coos of Thrush as he joins in the conversation. Noah laughs, the baby squeals. I force my eyes to close and try not to think how hard it must be for him to watch his son grow from afar. To watch the woman that he loves carry on with his brother. Noah got me in plenty of trouble when we were kids but I'm not sure anything will ever compete with the tangled relationship he's in with Nightingale.

At least they have each other. Sometimes.

I roll and tuck the blanket under my chin. Squeezing my eyes shut, I try to picture Sparrow in my mind. It's been months since I've seen him. I never had a picture, and the memories of him are turning into dark, blurry images. I tell myself that his eyes are as green as Ireland grass, his hair dark and shaggy, his stature tall and strong...

Damn.

LOST

SPARROW

Sparrow continued his walk down Redwood Highway. The Pacific waves had quieted, and Sparrow could hear the screams from the campsite as the walking sacks of dead flesh feasted. The morning chill was thick with fog. So much so that he couldn't even see the ocean anymore, only hear its gentle lapping against the rocky shoreline.

Footsteps followed him from the tree line. He ignored them. Someone had been following him for a long time. It wasn't the dead who had infested the Earthen plane. No, this was someone else, something else.

There was an empty car on the side of the highway. Thirsty, Sparrow tried the doorhandles. The passenger side opened. He dug through the car only to find empty water bottles and garbage. In the back there was an empty car seat. If Sparrow was of his right mind, he might've said a prayer for the child. Instead he walked away, leaving the car door open.

There were signs for a diner in two miles. He patted his pocket for the wad of cash he'd come across in his travels. His fingers brushed over the feather and the small hairs on the back of his neck rose. He rubbed his skin until they went away. He was hungry and he wasn't sure if food would fill the void. He wasn't sure if he could behave in the daylight.

Sparrow followed the signs and winding road. Footstep after footstep. Until he came to the diner.

Dan's Diner was an old building just off the highway, up on a slanted hillside with a wall of windows that overlooked the Pacific. Sparrow followed the incline of the crumbling driveway. The open sign was lit. He made his way to the door and went inside.

"Seat yourself," a voice shouted from the back.

The diner was empty. He chose a corner booth, where he could watch the door and the road.

A tattooed guy came out from the kitchen holding a menu. "Hey," he said, dropping the menu. "Can I get you a drink?"

Sparrow nodded. "Sure."

There was a long pause.

"What would you like?" the man asked.

"Anything."

"Water. Coffee. Soda?"

"Water," Sparrow said.

"No problem." The man reached forward and flipped the menu open. "There's no specials. Deliveries are too infrequent. Um. Hm. No steak or chicken. I've got a few eggs if you're looking for breakfast foods. No bacon though." He tapped on the menu. "We have fresh fish from the Pacific, some crab." He eyed Sparrow. "We have wonton soup but you're a big guy, you'll probably want something more filling than that."

Sparrow looked at the menu. Then the man's neck. His nametag said: Jed. He blinked and shook his head. He knew a Jed once. The name caused a buzzing in the back of his skull.

Jed took a step back. "How about this? I can whip you up a deep-fried grilled cheese and some eggs. Half price."

"Sure." Sparrow agreed and slid the menu in the man's direction. "I'll take an orange soda too if you have it." Orange soda reminded him of sweet lips and soft thighs.

"Coming right up," Jed said.

Sparrow watched out the window. There were no vehicles, no other people out walking on this misty morning. Well, besides whoever was waiting at the treeline. Only the shadow in the trees. For the first time in a long time it wasn't Sparrow.

Jed came back with a tall glass of orange soda and a water. "Ice machine is jammed."

"I don't need any." Sparrow drank the water first as Jed returned to the kitchen. He watched the trees and saw more of the woodpeckers with their bright red crests flitting back and forth. He had a desire to rip their wing feathers out, one by one, and rub them between his fingers. He could line his pockets with them. He could...

Jed set a plate in front of Sparrow. A steaming fried grilled cheese and large pile of eggs. Sparrow devoured the meal and drained both drinks, eager to get out of diner and move on. Eager to avoid the shadow in the trees and the pretty flitting songbirds. Eager to fill the void in his gut that the meal didn't touch. He needed more than food. But that would have to wait. He had no desire to drain Jed of his blood. Something about the guy was unappetizing.

Jed came back, a white slip of paper in his hand. Sparrow had his cash ready.

"I have a deal for you." Jed waved the paper. "Money is pretty useless these days. I need help with something, and we'll call the meal even."

Sparrow wiped his mouth with a napkin. "What is it?"

"I'll show you. Follow me."

Sparrow stood and followed Jed behind the counter, through the diner kitchen and to a silver door. Thuds were echoing from inside.

"I noticed your weapon." Jed motioned to Sparrow's blade. "I need them killed. I can't do it." Jed put his hand on the walk-in freezer door. "There's three of them."

Sparrow gripped his blade. "Why can't you do it?"

Jed pointed to a picture on the wall. "They owned this place. It just seems wrong. I can't."

Sparrow nodded and motioned for Jed to get out of the way. He took the handle to the door and pulled. There were three of the walking flesh-bags just like Jed said there'd be. They moved when they noticed him. Sparrow blocked the door so Jed couldn't see. The dead knew his darkness; they were just as lost as he was on the Earthen plane. Both didn't belong. Both were in limbo. But only one would stay. He'd send them away. For a free meal it was a decent trade.

Sparrow reached for his blade and in one swift movement relieved the dead of their heads. The smell was terrible: rotting flesh and rotting food. Sparrow stepped back and slammed the door closed. He walked to the sink to wash his hands and clean off his blade.

When Sparrow looked up, Jed was holding a butcher knife and standing near the back door to the diner. "Thank you for your help. Just go now." He pointed the butcher knife in the direction of the front door. "You're not one of those zombies, but you're something else. I remember. But you're worse than before. You've become something I've worked hard to avoid."

"Thanks for the meal." Sparrow turned and walked out the front door of the diner and continued on his way. He could have warned Jed about the swarm that would follow but he didn't.

No Rest for the Wicked

Meg

I dreamed of woodchucks, burrowing into the corner foundations of my house, gnawing away at the cement and wood and drywall. I filled their holes, sprinkled my foundation in fresh garlic. They still got in the house and scurried across the floorboards. I woke in my dream, a pinching feeling on my fingers and the blankets moving. I raised my hand to see a woodchuck bit me, teeth clamped in the soft spot between my thumb and index fingers. It dangled on the end of my hand, pinching my flesh. I gripped it under the arm with my free hand and the creature wiggled like a dachshund dog wanting to be put down. I ran to the slider door, kicked it open, and threw the woodchuck into the nearby pond. Fucking woodchucks.

I wake to a dark room, sweat soaking the satin sheets. Rubbing my face dry, I get up to use the bathroom.

I had a friend who once said, "I can't trust anyone. Not even a girl who can flash between realms and slay the walking dead like she was born and bred to take on the apocalypse single handedly." That was Jed. I'm not sure if he was truly a friend but he was a forbidden creature much like me. But damn him, he's the one who tattooed the runes into Sparrow's back with my own blood. He's the reason I can't find Sparrow.

I should find Jed. He should have warned me what a stupid idea it was to tattoo Sparrow so I'd never find him. It wasn't that long ago that I was *poofing* to his parlor, locking the doors in a desperate attempt to hide and asking him to help me.

"What are you thinking about, child?" Clea appears and the air turns chilled.

"Things," I reply. "Old things. Memories I can't seem to move on from."

Clea fidgets and paces, her image blurring to transparent and then returning solid again. Her dark flowing hair and ruby red lips are a stark contrast between her ghostly-white skin.

"What's wrong?" I ask.

"Have you thought any more about the basilisk?" she asks.

"Not really."

Skeele makes a noise from the corner of the room.

"What?" I ask.

"They come in handy," he says. "A basilisk is a powerful creature."

"So is a door. And I don't need a pet." I move to the balcony and set a row of seed out. "Besides, I wouldn't even know how to find one or catch it."

"Oh, there's a whole nest of them in the mountain streams," Clea says. "You just have to go hunt one."

"A nest of them." I shiver. "I'm not a fan of snakes, let alone giant snakes with teeth. I have no desire to hunt one. I'm trying to get out of here."

"You should have your house set before you venture out to the Earthen plane," Skeele warns.

"The Hellions are of no use while I'm gone?" I ask.

"A creature like the basilisk would give us a stronger edge," Skeele says.

"My grandfather's didn't. I sliced the guts out of that thing in an instant."

Skeele shrugs before leaving the room and muttering, "Think about it."

"Surround yourself with monsters," Clea warns before disappearing.

There are plenty of monsters in my life. I sit on the bed and glance at the jar of snowy owl feathers on my nightstand. They are all that remains of my daughter, Elise. There was a time in my life, before shit got real fucked up, when I was pregnant with a child. I didn't know my fiancée was the son of a demon, living on the Earthen plane. Heck, I didn't know what I was truly a product of. But Jim seduced me, knocked me up, and forever changed my life. Hellions made sure of this. Elise's soul rests now. She was two-thirds darkness and one-third light, the brightest light in the darkest of places. She was not meant for the Earthen plane, nor Hell. She was not meant for the slice of Lucifer's blade as she tried to defend me.

I pick up the jar and twist it to the side. The feathers fall softly. I don't want a basilisk. I want Sparrow. I want to get the heck out of Hell and roam the Earthen plane free as a bird.

Night Moves

Sparrow

Crescent City was quiet. The morning fog had cleared. Sparrow walked the main road toward the coast. People were out on boats and kayaks fishing. He took note of the houses. Many were boarded up. Sparrow needed to find someplace to hide until nightfall. He slowed his pace, listened to the hearts beating inside until he found a house that was empty and didn't look like anyone was coming back to it. Sparrow walked around the back, his boots disturbing dead leaves that had collected along the driveway. He found a back door, knocked. No one answered, just as he'd expected. He twisted the doorknob slowly; he met resistance but forced the knob until the mechanism inside broke with a snap. Sparrow let himself inside.

The house had been empty a long time. Probably before the dead started walking. There were holes in the wooden floorboards and a thick layer of dust coating everything. Sparrow found an old blanket next to the couch. He sat down, covered his knees and closed his eyes, ignoring the smell. He slept through the evening.

Sparrow left his hiding spot as soon as the sun went down.

Only half the streetlights were working and after spending so much time walking the unlit Redwood Highway, he was finding their brightness annoying. The few people still living in Crescent City avoided him, running into their houses and locking the doors or driving in another direction.

The breakfast he'd eaten at sunrise was doing nothing to stop the ache in his gut. Something else would stop it. Only one thing. He made his way toward the sound of loud music and the smell of stale beer.

The sign of the bar was unlit, bulbs had been shot out ages ago and these days there was no point in replacing them. Most of the people still living in Crescent City knew they were on borrowed time. There was no rhyme or reason when or where the swarm of the dead would show up–reports had shown destruction headed north up the California coast.

Sparrow hit the door and pushed it open. The bar quieted for a moment as he crossed the room and sat in a corner. Most soon forgot him but a leery eye was quick to judge.

"What can I get you?" a woman wearing a Crescent City Dodgeball T-shirt asked.

"Whatever you have on tap," Sparrow replied.

"Uh huh." The woman stared at him. "You look new to town. Don't try any funny business. These boys don't have much of a reason not to shoot you." She thrust her thumb toward a group of men playing pool.

The corner of Sparrow's mouth rose as the woman turned to get his beer. When she came back, she slid a mug of the house special on tap slowly. Sparrow let his fingers touch hers as he took the mug. That was all he needed to do. It didn't take much for women to bend to his needs.

The woman in the dodgeball shirt kept his mug full and the people of the bar kept Sparrow entertained. Music played, got louder as the night went on, then migrated from classic rock to body swaying rave music. Sparrow got up to use the bathroom.

Walking past the sweaty bodies with their heartbeats thundering was almost too much. Almost. He used the stall, washed his hands, and splashed cold water on his face and neck. He was lost, fighting an urge that was only quelled by walking away from everyone he came across. It was that or give in. Walk away or give in? Which was more dangerous? Which would put an end to the ache? He had a void that needed filled. Now.

Sparrow left the bathroom. His heavy footsteps were drowned out by the loud music. He watched a young woman in a low-cut blue shirt dancing. She had short dark hair, fair skin, ink decorating her shoulder blades. She caught him watching, spun and grabbed his arm.

"Dance," she shouted with a wide smile.

A pang of memories hit. Memories of a dark-haired woman covered with tattoos of him. A woman with blue eyes who only saw him. Sparrow could bury it and dance. He closed his eyes, felt the music loosen his muscles. The woman was close to him, touching him, her small hand resting on his hip as she rubbed her body on his. Sparrow looked down at her with half-lidded eyes. She smiled, tipped her head to the side and bared her neck. Someone knocked into his back and pushed them closer together. She reached out, took his hand and placed it on her hip as one song merged into another that was just as loud and upbeat. He squeezed her waist. He couldn't hear the words, couldn't focus on anything other than the pulse in her neck. He tipped his head, pressed his lips to the vee of her neck.

"Yes," she whispered in his ear.

Teeth bared, he settled them over her carotid. She kept dancing, her arms circling his waist, pulling them closer together.

Sparrow bit down and tasted blood for the first time in days. He wrapped his arms around the woman, held her up while he drained her. She never struggled. Her blood was heavy with alcohol, and something else. Drugs, maybe? The bloodlust was too strong to ignore. It didn't bother him that she was inebriated. He let go and she dropped to the ground, an empty sack of skin. The dark, crowded room barely noticed. Sparrow moved like a shadow across the room, feeding on one and then the next until someone finally realized what he was doing. There were screams. Gun shots fired but barely nicked him. What did, healed in an instant. The room filled with panic. A few screams echoed but fell upon a closed door. It was soon locked and covered in bloody handprints.

When Sparrow left the bar, there were no hearts beating. He let the door to the bar close behind him, wiped his mouth on the back of his hand, and walked away. The streetlights near the bar went out.

The hoard of the dead echoed from nearby. After they passed, they'd clean up his mess. No one on the Earthen plane would know what he'd done here.

Fishin' in the Dark

"Find the basilisk." My father is suddenly in the room. He is the brightest light in this place, shining through all the shadows. I wonder if this is what Clea meant when she described my child's light. My child that never was.

"Jesus Christ." I hold a hand over my heart. "You scared the shit out of me."

"That's no way to greet good 'ol dad." He smiles wide.

"How did you get here?" I ask.

He throws his hands in the air. "Magic."

"We both know it's not magic."

He pauses at the doors to the balcony. "True." His fingers fall on the doorhandle. "Only a few of us have the gift to travel between realms on a whim."

"They'll see you," I warn him. "And I'm pretty sure that you're not supposed to be here right now."

He clears his throat. "I was sent. The Seven Kingdoms of Heaven sent me to speak with you."

"How nice of them. No one else wanted to come down

here?" I flash a mocking smile and bat my eyes innocently. "I've got my own cages now." I don't need to remind him of how they treated me in Heaven; locked me in a cage in the hot burning sun and let the angels judge me. My blood boils with the memory.

Heavy footsteps pound down the hall outside my door.

My father's brows rise in interest. "This could get fun after all."

"Not today, you celestial punk." I dash toward the door and pull it open just in time, before six giant Hellions bust it down. "Stop," I warn them. "I just got this door fixed. Do not enter here."

"Meg," Skeele argues. He's gripping a club. I glance over the Hellions; they've all got weapons.

"No." My hand grips the door handle. "You can stay out here, but do not enter this room."

Klaus sniffs the air. "It doesn't belong here," he growls.

Skeele raises a hand to stop the others. "We'll wait here."

"Of course you will." I retreat to my room and close the door.

"I figured you'd have more... protection." My father wanders the room before sitting on the bed.

"There's enough." I wave toward the door.

"You should have more." His fingers smooth over the dark bedspread. "Is your mother here?"

"Yes. Is that who you came to see?" I ask.

He pauses. "I suppose it's not the best idea to rip open old wounds."

"Probs not." I sit in a chair and glance at the door. The powerful aura of the Hellions is spilling into the room. We'd have to be dead not to feel it. Their heated rage could melt a statue.

"Are you aware of the missing souls?" my father asks.

"I'm not sure what you mean. There are a lot coming here and we've had backup in productivity at the Safe Houses."

He's shaking his head. "No. There's something more than

that. They aren't even leaving the Earthen plane. They're walking around it. Dead."

"Oh." I remember those days, escaping the stinking flesh bags while I was hiding in Key West. "Heaven didn't seem to give a crap before when the Scarecrow was dropping zombies on the Earthen plane to toy with me."

"This is much different. The balance is so far out of whack..." he shakes his head. "They want to hold you responsible."

"Don't they always." I sigh, bored with the same old conversation. *It's Meg's fault. Punish Meg. Lock Meg up in some shitty dungeon and make her pay.* You'd think a group of Archangels would have a real strategy.

"I told them to fuck off." He laughs. "You should have seen the look on Raguel's face." Large hands clap. "Once in a lifetime. But, probably not."

"Sounds like a real great time."

He catches his breath. "You have to go to the Earthen plane and fix it."

"I know but I can't leave here. The Veil prevents me from leaving."

"Everyone knows about the solstice." He blurts out as though he's read my mind. "That's your time to go."

"You make it sound so easy." I mock.

"There's another way to go."

"Oh?" Now he's got my interest.

"Unless you relinquish the throne."

"Nah." I shake my head. "I won't be doing that." After all I've gone through why would I stand down now?

"Good. The solstice is a better choice. But, you need this." He reaches in his shirt pocket and pulls out a small vial of red liquid.

"What is that?" My mouth salivates. I already know. Blood.

"Consider it a gift."

I step back, afraid I won't keep it together around the blood.

My veins sing at the sight, vibrating with anticipation. I thoroughly enjoyed the tang of Remiel's and Lucifer's blood.

He holds up the vial. "The blood of your father. It will mask you on the Earthen plane. But not for long. With this and the solstice you should get a good start." He stands. "Well, I guess that's enough chit-chat. Will you be coming with me?" He frowns. "I'd hate to see you locked up in the burning sun again." He pats a large hand over his heart. "Really made me want to kick some ass like never before."

"No." I shake my head. "I'm not ever going back there."

"Good, kid. I'll tell Raguel he can go fuck himself."

"Please do."

Gabriel laughs loudly, reaches across the table, and slaps me on the shoulder. "You've done good kid. Made a name for yourself and all." He surveys the room and the balcony. "Better than where you started off. I'm glad we found you."

"Thanks... Dad. Do I call you dad or father or something more?" I ask.

"Don't be a stranger." He waves before *poofing* back to Heaven.

I grab my jacket off the back of the chair, hide the jar of blood in a drawer, and cross the room. When I open the door, the Hellions are a wall of energy, barely holding back. Skeele looks ready to kill.

"He's gone," I say. "Calm down."

"What did he want?" Tukka asks, sniffing the room like a guard dog.

"To pass along information," I reply.

The Hellions push their way into my room and begin searching.

"I told you all he's gone." I wave toward the sky. "He went back to where he lives." I open and close the door to make sure it's really there and really works and isn't a figment of my imagination. "Do you all know what this thing is?" I wiggle the door, annoyed.

Skeele crosses his arms. "You shouldn't lock us out when one of his kind are here."

"He's my father," I say.

Skeele tips his head and narrows his eyes. "Family are the most likely to do harm."

I pause. Sure as shit they are. Memories of the man who raised me flood my mind. I put my jacket on and rest my hand on the doorknob. "We ready boys?"

"For what?" Skeele asks.

"Hunting basilisk," I say.

Only Skeele and Tukka came with me. The others said since I killed one basilisk, collecting another will be a piece of cake. We walk out of the front door and load into the Jeep Wrangler. Skeele drives, Tukka crams himself in the back with a large reed basket.

Skeele heads north, toward what would be the Adirondack mountains on the Earthen plane. I guess they're the Adirondack mountains here too, just a darkened reflection.

"What do you think Sparrow is doing?" I ask Skeele.

"Something... weird."

I smile. "He's like that. Worse when he forgets who he is."

Skeele grunts in agreement.

"I have to go to him," I say. "I must do this. Then I'll go. Finally."

"Making a list." Skeele gets a tick in his cheek. "It's about time."

"What do you think he's surviving on?" I ask.

"Blood." Skeele is frank in the reply.

"Not mine."

"Nope."

Of course, he's feeding off others. He has too. I can't hold it against him, can I? I can't expect him to be traipsing across the

United States without a spec of grace on an empty stomach. Who does that? What creature of Hell could have the strength to do that? I doubt I could.

"Stop thinking so hard about it," Skeele warns.

"Okay." I gaze at the passing forest.

"Maybe this is a good time to try flying again," Skeele says.

I hold my hands up and lean against the back of my seat. "I don't think this is a good time."

"Come on, Meg. Maybe just, jump off a big rock or out of a tree. Scare yourself a little." Tukka chuckles.

"You're something special, aren't you?" I ask.

Tukka shrugs. "I'm just a Hellion doing his job."

"No more from the peanut gallery," I warn Tukka.

"I'm not a peanut."

I turn and look out the passenger side window again. "You're definitely not." My stomach growls and I think about the vial of my father's blood that I left in my room.

"You want to stop and eat?" Skeele asks.

"Not right now. Just keep going," I reply. "I'll eat something later."

I can't deal with my stomach right now. I'll do what I've been doing for months. Binge on snacks, feel like crap, and in a moment of weakness give in to the bagged blood. It's a vicious cycle.

Skeele drives from Scranton to Old Forge via Interstate-81. There's no traffic, and we are the only vehicle on the highway. We pass herds of the walking dead. As we get close, they move away. It's a nice change from them coming after me and trying to eat my face. We pass pine forests and rocky cutouts. The further north we get, the more I remember my travels with Sparrow before we knew who we were. Although, the guy has so many issues with his brain I'm sure he's forgotten everything again. I long for the days in which we can just be ourselves. I'll take him either way though, a Sparrow who knows who I am is just as good as a Sparrow who has no clue. He's fun either way, and nice to look at.

Skeele pulls off the exit toward Interstate-481 north then Interstate-90 east. We pass forests and farmland. A few people run and hide as we pass. There's a man at the mailbox. He opens it and looks a few times. There's no mail delivery in Hell, must be a habit that stuck. He runs down the driveway when he sees us coming. There's a woman in an open field. She's picking black-eyed-susans and looking up at the sky. As we pass she drops below the tall field grass. It seems most of the souls here act slightly confused and reminiscent of their lives on the Earthen plane. I remember when that was me.

"They haven't figured it out yet," Skeele says.

"I've been there," I reply.

Skeele nods. "We all have. If you're dropped in a dead zone with no signs, it can take a long time to figure things out."

"How many people do you think are down here and dead without knowing it?" I ask.

"Plenty," Skeele says. "Basilisk den isn't far from here. There's a cave near the Black River."

"Wonderful." I shift in my seat, trying not to act anxious.

Skeele merges onto 365 E and veers off onto Eastern Rock Rd. "Avoiding the locals," he says as I reach for the door to steady myself on the bumpy road.

The road ends behind an old Tops grocery store. Skeele jerks the wheel to the left to avoid a walking sack of flesh, rounds a garbage dumpster, and takes a right. He drives for a block before turning right again onto Moose River Road.

"What's wrong?" Skeele asks.

"I'm fine." I don't care to tell him that this place reminds me of Gouverneur where I grew up. The busted roads, dingy old houses, and grocery stores barely held together bring back the sadness of life in a small northern town. Defeat hits a person early, around elementary school age when you know you'll probably never get out unless a miracle happens. You hunker down and prep yourself for a hard life of minimum wage jobs, high taxes, a shitload of snow in the winter and frozen water pipes. You'll be cold and angry and sad and settle for the subpar.

I can see the Black River from the road. Skeele points to the slick serpentine backs of the basilisk swimming in the river. I shiver.

"How many of them are here?" I ask.

"Plenty," Skeele replies. "They spawn here throughout the year."

"Remember, you only need one," Tukka says.

"One is more than I'd like." I settle my hand over the blade at my thigh. "The last basilisk I met I killed. Somehow, I have to get one of these back to my castle alive and train it."

"It can be done," Skeele says. "Lucifer did it."

The road turns winding, with the riverbank just a few feet away. Skeele pulls over and parks on an outcropping of sand.

"Let's get this over with," I say as I open the door and step out.

Tukka jumps out from the rear passenger side and reaches over the door to get the basket as Skeele rounds the front of the Jeep. We walk through the row of pine trees and out onto a giant boulder. The river is filled with basilisk, large and small, serpentine bodies wavering under the current of cold water. If I didn't know better, I'd simply think the water was dark black and filled with current.

"There are small ones?" I point upstream to a shallow area with about ten basilisk that are no longer than five or six foot long. "I can just take a small one."

"It's not that easy," Skeele says. "Those are babies. You can take a baby, but you'll have to face the mother. She'll come after you."

"Oh?" I move closer to the shallow pool of the river.

"There," Tukka says as he points to the center of the river.

I look up to see a giant head has risen from the surface of the river. Rows of sharp teeth hiss in my direction.

"Do you think that's the mother?" I shout back to the guys as I jump down from the boulder.

"I'm going to guess it is," Skeele says.

I run toward the pool of babies. The mother starts to swim closer, teeth bared.

"Wait for us, Meg," Skeele shouts.

Footsteps follow behind me. I grip my blade and stop at the edge of the pool. The mother is directly across from me.

"Toss me the basket," I order Tukka.

He throws it and it plops into the pool. The baby basilisk barely flinch.

"They don't seem scared," I say as I secure my blade, crouch down, and reach into the cold water.

"Just remember, a baby basilisk won't protect your castle until it's older," Skeele says.

I want the mother. Mothers follow one thing, their children. Looks like I'm about to get a basilisk family.

"I guess we'll take them all." I reach further into the water and scoop up a baby basilisk and put it in the reed basket. The mother's head and body start to come out of the water.

"What's your plan, Meg?" Skeele asks.

"We take them all, and she follows."

Boots thud behind me as Skeele hops down from his perch on the rock and starts helping me collect the babies.

"These things are gross," I say as I rinse the slimy ruminants off my hand with the river water.

"Don't think about it," Skeele says.

We get all the babies but three that are further back. I take off my jacket and toss it on the riverbank before I slip into the water, sliding my feet across the rocky pool, scoop them up and put them in the basket.

When I look up again, the mother is a foot from my face. A hundred tiny, sharp teeth greet me. I scramble back, grab the basket, and toss it up on the riverbank. Tukka grabs the basket as it tips to the side, slams the lid closed and locks it. The babies shriek and it is ear piercing. Skeele grabs the back of my jeans and tugs me out of the water. "What's your plan?" he asks as I stumble and grab my jacket off the ground.

"A mother follows her babies. So, we better run home as fast as we can," I say, out of breath.

We run toward the Jeep. The baby basilisk writhe and screech and Tukka's muscles bulge as he does his best to keep ahold of the basket as it shifts with their movement.

I turn and find the mother following us. "I hope you can drive faster than she slithers," I shout to Skeele.

He jumps behind the wheel just as Tukka loads the basket and jumps over the rear gate to get into the back of the Jeep. I scramble inside and lock the door.

"Go go go!" we all shout in unison.

"She won't just slither," Skeele says as he slams his foot down on the gas. "She can kinda fly."

"Like with wings?" I ask.

"Not really. It kinda floats in the air and water," Tukka says.

"Why in the hell does everything down here fly except me?" I ask.

Tukka breaks out in laughter from the back seat.

"What?" I ask.

"The dead don't fly," he says.

"Give it time. I'm sure they will soon." I glance behind us and sure as shit the basilisk is floating above the asphalt.

"See, that wasn't so bad, was it?" Skeele asks.

"When you all told me I had to capture a basilisk, I figured I was going to have to fight it or play the flute to hypnotize it," I say.

Skeele drives fast as heck to get us back to the castle, the mother about half a mile behind us the entire time. Always watching. Always moving. She never stops pursuing us.

"What are you going to do with the babies?" Tukka asks. "Kill them now that you'll have the mother?"

"No," I say. That would be cruel. And while I am many things, I don't think I could live with myself for being cruel to a mother. The jar of feathers on my nightstand is a testament to that.

"Noah!" I shout.

It takes a few minutes for him to appear.

"Yes, your highness," he asks as he bows.

"I need a big fish tank."

"Please don't tell me you want live fish fry." Noah makes a disgusted face.

"No, I need a giant tank set up in Lucifers office for the basket 'o basilisk babies." I point.

Noah looks to my Hellions and the babies in the basket screech on que.

"Oh, of all the bullshit you get me into. Okay. Give me a minute." Noah disappears.

As we head to the front door, the mother turns down the curve in the road.

"Leave the door open," I say.

We make our way to the office. Doors slam as the basilisk mother enters the building. There's a few growls and the scattering sound of small shadow creatures running away.

Noah is already setting up a huge tank when we get there. It's already filled with water. Noah plugs a cord into the wall and a small octopus decoration emits bubbles from inside the tank.

"Let's get the babies in," I say.

Tukka sets the basket down and we take turns grabbing the slimy babies and getting them into the tank. It's a struggle with their long bodies and writhing.

"Oh lord," Noah whispers. "Those are nasty."

We turn to see the mother's head peeking through the door, large beady eyes and knife sharp teeth. She stares at me as she enters the room, sizing me up. I point to the dark ceiling where my grand-father kept his basilisk. Knowing, she slithers through the air and coils herself against the ceiling.

"Don't forget to feed the babies," Tukka whispers.

"What do they eat?" I ask as we walk out of the room.

"I am not in charge of that chore," Noah complains. "Feeding Meg is hard enough."

"Spinach and crawfish," Skeele says as we leave the room and close the door.

"I'm not sure I'll ever go back in there," I say. "It's all you, Noah."

"You have to train them all," Skeele reminds me.

I shudder. "I need a drink."

We walk down to the Hellions lair. I run to the sink and wash the slime off my hands. When I turn around, the whole crew is watching me.

"What?" I ask.

"You went to get one basilisk and come back with an entire family," Klaus says. "Never seen the ruler of Hell do that before."

I shrug. "What can I say?"

Keep On

Sparrow

Sparrow headed north, again. He was moving so fast he was nearly flying. The urge was there, the memory, but he didn't have wings on the Earthen plane. What he wouldn't give to spread them out and stretch with a gut full of blood. It would have been exhilarating.

Sparrow left Crescent City quick enough for the dead to clean up his mess. No one would suspect much at the bar after they see the rest of the town. Sometimes having a horde of the dead trailing you is a good thing. Well, good for Sparrow in the sense it hid his tracks from the unsuspecting.

The Redwood Highway swayed inland and took Sparrow's view of the ocean, the clash of the waves, and without them he could hear the garbled sounds of the walking dead taking over Crescent City. He moved faster, eager to escape the noise, knowing they'd be following him as soon as they were done.

When the moon was directly overhead, headlights lit the highway from behind him. A caravan of those who were lucky enough to escape were coming. They honked as they passed.

"Get out of the road!" someone shouted. Trucks spilling with people passed. Cars weighed down with families and supplies sped by. Their eyes were wide as they passed Sparrow, their heads turning in awe that he was merely walking alone and not running like them.

A vehicle lingered behind. Sparrow moved to the other lane and slowed. A Jeep Wrangler, with the top off turned in front of him and stopped.

Sparrow grabbed his blade, holding it out at arm's length. He was met with the rounded end of a baseball bat. He looked past it and recognized the woman from the forest with blue hair.

"You going to slice me up with that?" she asked.

"If I need to," Sparrow replied. "You going to bludgeon me with that?" he nodded toward the bat.

"If I need to," she replied with a smirk. "You want a ride?"

Sparrow looked past her and recognized Jed from the diner in the passenger seat.

"I like to walk." Sparrow secured his blade.

"There's blood on you." She motioned to his hand and face.

Sparrow wiped at his mouth with an open palm. "Got in a fight."

Her eyes narrowed and Jed whispered something. "I bet you won. Seem the type."

Sparrow smiled; it was arrogant and dark. "I always do."

Something fell out of the sky and landed at Sparrow's feet with a thud.

"What the heck?" the blue haired woman made a face.

Sparrow bent and picked up the dead bird. "It's a raven." Sparrow stroked the feathers. His fingers petted the thick flight feathers at the base of its wings. He gripped two and tugged hard, pulling them out. He tucked them in his pocket before gently setting down the carcass off the side of the road. He dug a small hole in the dirt with his hands and buried the creature. The eerie sound of a dozen crows cawing from the power lines filled the night.

"I'd get a move on. The dead are following." The chick in the Jeep pressed down on the gas pedal and began driving away.

"They always do," Sparrow said as he stood and looked up. There were more dead ravens, more feathers went into his pockets–some he didn't have the urgency to bury.

An unkindness of ravens above him cawed louder.

Nightmares

MEG

I'm flying, really flying. My wings spread and soak up the sepia light of Hellsky. Something hits me from behind, wraps its arms and legs around me. I fight. I bite. I tear whatever it is to pieces. My wings are suddenly gone. I drop from the sky like a sack of shit. Just like the night after draining Lucifer dry and I fell to the ground and broke every bone in my body.

I wake in a pool of sweat. I rub my arms and legs, making sure it was just a dream. It was just a dream. Damn you, Nightingale. I need these dreams to end. I wake more tired than the night before.

"It wasn't me," a familiar voice says.

In the darkness of the room, I see nothing.

"Where are you?" I ask.

"In between the Astral and your land." The sound of a baby cooing interrupts her.

"Are you..."

"Don't ask." Her voice is firm. "I just stopped by to remind you that the winter solstice is upon us. The extended hours of darkness will part the veil. It's how I used to sneak out of Heaven."

"You used to sneak out?" I ask.

"Sparrow was the only good one." There is a long pause. "I miss him, Meg. You must go find him."

"I'll find him," I promise. I hope it's not a lie. I have to find him.

"We only had him back for a short time." The sorrow in her voice is thick. "I'd like him to meet his nephew."

"He's a Hellion now," I remind her.

"It doesn't matter. He's still my brother. He's still doing his best to be a curse breaker."

"Okay, Night," I promise again. "I'm going to find him, even if it kills me."

"Be safe, Meg. We love you."

She's gone and I'm left with the echo of her words. Never has anyone said that to me. Besides Sparrow, but he must. He's required to say things like that. But not Nightingale. Not anyone else in my life. I throw the covers back and move to get out of bed. If the winter solstice is here, then I'm not waiting one second longer. I got the Basilisk. I glance at the nightstand drawer. I've got the blood of an Archangel.

I head to the bathroom to shower, knowing it might be a very long time until I get to shower again. I scrub and shave like I'm getting ready for prom. When Sparrow sees me again, I'd like to be all shiny and clean for him. I towel off, realizing that I'm going to miss the luxuries I have here. It didn't take long to get used to them, even though I lived without for most of my life.

I get dressed in the closet, selecting jeans, a T-shirt with a wide neck and a dark blue canvas jacket. I dig around until I find my old backpack with the single strap. I fill it with a change of clothes and clean underwear.

"Noah," I beckon. "Noah, I need you to get me some things."

The room chills as Noah arrives. "Are we taking a trip?"

"I am. Hey, I need you to get me a big canteen with fresh water, some granola bars and protein bars. Maybe some survival gear if you can find it."

"Sounds like you're going camping."

"Not camping. But if the Earthen plane is anything like it was last time the dead were walking around there, I need to prepare myself to walk into some apocalyptic bullshit."

"Look at you having all the fun. I'm jealous."

I pause, feeling guilty. Noah died; his soul is trapped in the Astral plane. At least that is an unruled plane, at least he and Nightingale can see each other there. I'd love nothing more than for him to come with me. "Sorry," I say.

"No biggie." He waves it off. "I'll go get your survival crap."

After he leaves, I dig out a pair of thick socks, add a second pair to my bag. I put on my leather hiking boots. There's still mud caked to them from mine and Sparrow's previous travels. It feels weird gearing up to walk into Hell. Well, not my Hell; a different type of Hell. America being torn apart by the dead as they eat their way across the continent. This sounds like the crappiest trip I've ever planned. The only bright side is finding Sparrow and bringing him home.

Home. There was a time when home was all I wanted. When I traipsed across upstate NY in search of a home nothing felt right, no matter where I landed. It didn't matter if I was going back to that white house with a green door and picket fence. I did my best to make that my home but it never stuck. I learned why in the worst way possible. I learned who I was and what I'd come from. But now, being here in Hell and knowing the rules and who makes them, knowing the flow of Heaven and Hell and the Earthen plane; now I finally feel at home. I will feel even more at home with Sparrow here. Just like Nightingale said, we miss him.

There's a noise in my bedroom. I step out of the closet and find Noah piling what he found onto my bed.

"Hey," he nods as he stacks protein bars and sets the canteen upright.

"Look at this." I toss my backpack on the bed and unzip it.

"You might have to remove some clothes to make this fit."

"I only packed one outfit."

"Maybe a bigger pack?"

"No." I shake my head. "I get the feeling I'm going to be running, a lot, and I can't be doing that with a huge pack on my back."

Noah whistles a trill as he scratches his head. I guess he picked that up from Nightingale. I've only seen Night and Sparrow communicate with birdsong.

I stack the bars and snacks and tuck them into my bag. "They'll be eaten before I know it," I say. "There's no point in leaving food behind. I'll be starving. Half of it will be gone in twenty-four hours."

Noah chuckles. "Hey, my girl likes to eat."

"I'm not your girl."

Noah raises his arms in defense. "Used to be." His brow rises and he smirks.

"Shut up."

Noah rubs his pinched fingers over his lips like he's zipping them closed.

I open the nightstand and take out the vial of my father's blood.

"What's that?" Noah asks.

"Nothing." I push it into my pocket, my mouth salivating at the thought of drinking it.

I pick up the canteen and weigh it in my hand. There's a strap to hold it or a clip. It's too heavy to clip to my pack. I've been on the road with nothing before. Just a nearly empty bag and scavenging from house to house. This packing session feels very hoity-toity and I'm ready to toss the bag and walk through the veil with nothing more than my blade and a prayer to Bon Jovi.

"You're right," Noah says.

"You read minds now too?" I ask.

"I can read you. You don't need all this stuff. I get the feeling you'll be tossing it all on the side of the road before you get very far."

"I might." I agree with him. "But I guess I should put forth the effort to pack for once in my life."

"If that's a goal of yours, I'd say you're there."

I smile. "Thanks, Noah."

He sits and stretches his arms behind his head. "I'm so ready for this vacation. No more running for food. It will be just me and this balcony and the birds."

"Boring." I toss a pillow at him. "You punk."

Noah catches the pillow. "I know you'll miss me."

I adjust the backpack strap and put it over my shoulder. "Don't forget to feed the Basilisk and its babies."

A groan of disapproval erupts from Noah. "Dear God, no."

"Hey, they're our pets now."

"I did not agree to this."

"Neither did I." I laugh as I leave the room.

<hr>

The Hellion's lair is humming with wild energy. I knock on the door, warning them that I'm about to enter.

"You're up early," Skeele says as I enter.

"I should have never gone to sleep," I say.

"Where are you going?" Klaus asks, smoothing his beard with both hands. I notice all their batlike wings are folded taut behind their backs.

"It's time for me to go," I say.

Skeele is behind the bar, pouring packet blood into glasses. "One for the road?" he asks, his curled horns reflecting the overhead lights.

I pause, close my eyes, and nod. There's no denying that I'll need it for what I'm about to walk into.

"One of us should go with you," Tukka says. "From what I've heard it's absolute chaos on the Earthen plane right now."

"I don't think that's necessary." I pat the blade at my leg. "I'll be just fine."

"You still can't fly," Skeele points out.

"That doesn't matter. None of us can fly on the Earthen plane." I take the few steps to the bar and pick up the glass Skeele slides toward me.

"If the conditions are right, we can," Tukka says. "There's stories about it."

Skeele shushes Tukka. "Those are stories. That's it. The rules between realms are clear."

I down the blood, my body sings with relief. It's been weeks since I last gave in. I quell the lust and direct my brain elsewhere.

"I need a ride to the portal before the sun rises." I lick my lips, not wasting a drop.

"We'll take you," Skeele says as he waves for Tukka to follow.

"Good luck," Chel says from the shadows of the room.

We leave the dark castle built into the burning caves and walk toward the Jeep. A shadow covers the dull moonglow, I look up to see Clea as the argentavis flying above us. Skeele drives and Clea follows from overhead. The ride to the field with the portal is quick. As Skeele parks I notice the wavering shadows around the portal. Creatures slither back and forth.

"What are they doing?" I ask.

"Collecting things. Escaping." Skeele gets out and grips his blade. It glows and hums. The shadowed things scatter, and I see the extent of the parted veil around the portal.

"When you pass, it will rip further," Tukka says. "It won't be closed completely until you return. Or time runs out."

"So those creatures and souls can still leak out?" I ask.

"Yup." Skeele slaps a fancy cellphone into my hand.

"For the love of all that is holy, I do not want this thing," I complain as I press a button and check the battery.

"All the cool kids are carrying one, and it might come in handy while you're looking for bird boy." Skeele says.

"You're not coming?" I ask, testing.

Skeele smirks. "When have you ever needed help? Especially from a Hellion?"

I weight the phone in my palm. "I need a navigator for this pile of crap." With each year I age technology seems to escape me a little more.

"You'll figure it out." Skeele chuckles as he walks away.

I fully expected one of them to come with me, but I don't need them. I don't really want them. They are a distraction. I need to focus on one thing. Finding Sparrow.

I stand in front of the portal, Clea flying overhead, my Hellions waiting in the darkness. I take a deep breath.

I accept that I am bred of monsters. I am a monster, bloodthirsty and damned. The blood of the Archangel Michael and Lucifer pumps through my veins, and soon the pureblood of Gabriel. I remove the vial from my pocket and down it. Power rushes through my veins. I will miss the smell of woodsmoke and pine.

"I'm coming for you, Sparrow," I whisper into the night.

SNOW ASH

MEG

I exit the portal at a church in Pennsylvania. Prince of Peace Roman Catholic Church, the sign states. Its peaks are five stories tall. The windows are dark but I notice the gothic decorations in the early morning light. Gargoyles stare down at me.

I pull my coat tighter and kick at the snow that's built up on the cement steps. It didn't take me long to forget about winters of the Earthen plane. I grip the strap of my bag and walk down the steps. The early morning is eerie. There are no cars on the street and no one walking to work or school. Down the road I see a convenience store and walk toward it. The heavy canteen knocks against the back of my leg. That's going to have to go. I stop in front of a newspaper machine, pull down the handle and take out a fresh paper.

I didn't think I'd been gone from the Earthen plane for long, but it appears everything here has fallen apart.

"Oh God," I mutter to myself as I read the front-page story about a hoard of zombies eating their way up the coast of California. There's a picture of a highway by the sea and a burning sign. I keep reading. There's been outbreaks in every state. I turn the page and read about safe areas, how to stock up on weapons and food, and how to kill a sack of walking flesh. It seems they're taking this seriously. Too bad it won't stop until I get Sparrow in the correct realm.

The Scarecrow told us that Sparrow's last bit of grace was disrupting the fiber between Hell and the Earthen plane. But this seems extreme. Not long ago the Coast Guard and Military were able to secure the dead outbreaks. Now, it seems it's all gone to hell.

Shuffling feet interrupt my reading. I turn and find myself face to face with a dead man. He growls and decaying jaws snap open and closed.

I drop the paper, grab my blade and slice his head off. It rolls to the ground and his body drops, jaws still snapping for a few more seconds. His teeth are clanking together, hoping for a bite of fresh flesh.

"Gross." I clean my blade on the corpses clothes and secure it again.

I need to find shelter and think. I grab the newspaper off the melting snow and look toward the door of the convenience store. A woman inside is watching me. The doors are chained closed. She shakes her head no. I'm shit out of luck here in PA.

I pull the phone out of my pocket. Tap, tap, tap the screen but nothing happens. I hold it up in the air. There's no service. Damn. I told Skeele I didn't need this piece of junk.

I start walking and thinking. I grip the newspaper tighter in my hand. As I walk through the valley of the shadow of death, I realize that I can't always trust in Google maps. There's nothing here. Sparrow isn't here. Even though he's tattooed skull to tailbone in runes to hide him, I'd know. I'd have to know. That newspaper was a sign from... someone. I glance at the sky. This is God's land, but he's never helped me before. Maybe he's truly tired of us mucking it up? I no longer teeter on the fringes of belonging here. All I can figure is he wants us out. I don't have much time.

Poof.

I go to California.

I travel to the picture from the newspaper. The waves crashing drown out all sound. It's still dark here, the only light coming from the glow of the moon. I grip my blade, crouch, and take in my surroundings. Maybe I *should* have brought a Hellion with me. I've never been to California. Who knows the kind of horrors that lurk here?

I start walking.

California is just like every TV show from 2010. Tall pines, sea salt spray from the ocean, fancy cars. I focus on the abandoned Mercedes in front of me. There's a corpse behind the wheel. I blink a few times until my eyes adjust and remember Sparrow's rule from so long ago: cars make noise, noise brings the dead, we walk. Sure that there's no one nearby, I head north. I tuck the newspaper into the side pocket of my bag and release the canteen. I can't stand it whacking against my leg for one more minute.

I stay close to the guardrail of the road so I can see anything coming out of the forest on the other side. I weave around abandoned and broken cars. My stomach growls. That didn't take long. I tell myself that I'll have a snack when I get to the next road sign that tells me where I am. As I walk, the sky lightens and the chilled night air warms. A few crows lift from the nearby trees. I know one thing. Where there are birds, there is Sparrow. I pick up my pace, walking for a good hour before I come to a sign letting me know I'm on Redwood Highway. I pull out my phone and try to get it to work. There's another sign for DeMartin Campsite, and nearby Crescent City. The power icon circles on the screen. I give up too easily. I got by for plenty of years without a cell phone. I tuck it in my pocket, my finger swiping over the empty vial of blood. Later I'll eat something, I tell myself. Save the energy bars for later. I can do this without them. It's just walking. No fighting. No drama. I tap the empty vial and remove my hand from my pocket.

There's noise in the forest. Boots crunching over dried sticks and pine needles interrupts the early morning hours. And... a pulsing sound. I can smell blood that's unspilled. I can hear the pulsing of a handful of people. My mouth waters. I guess this is what I get for stepping into my grandfather's boots. Bloodlust and all the rest. At least I get a heads up that I'm not alone. Someone is watching me from the treeline.

"Are you alive?" a man's voice whispers.

"Mostly," I reply.

"Do you need help?" he asks.

"Nope." I keep walking and consider walking faster.

A guy steps out into the road.

"I'm just traveling through," I say.

"We have food."

If only he knew, he's food to me. "I'm fine." I grip my blade. "I'm just crossing thru these parts."

"You talk different." His eyes narrow on me.

"At least I talk."

The guy motions to the road ahead. "A whole heard of the dead came by these parts not too long ago. You won't find anyone alive."

I stare.

"Can I come with you?" he asks.

There's a bite mark on his neck. The teeth marks are black, the blackness spreading away from the wound like ice cracks.

"No," I reply as I think to relieve him of his head before he turns.

"Please." The desperation in his voice is terrible. He walks closer.

I point my blade in his direction. "Go live out the last of your days. Leave me alone."

That guy will be a walking sack of flesh in no time. I pick up my pace. He stands still and watches me go. I walk faster than I'd like too, glad that I stuck to my guns and kept the small pack and didn't switch to a bigger one like Noah suggested.

A good long time goes by before I see a sign that tells me I'm still on Redwood Highway. Crescent City is a few miles ahead and Demartin Campground is the next exit.

I never was much of a camping person. Sleeping on the hard ground in a nylon tent never sounded appealing to me. I can imagine there's plenty of people on the run these days. But a tent, no, you couldn't drag me into a tent to sleep for the night. I'd rather sleep on a floating door in the ocean.

Crescent City is empty. There's barely any cars and the ones I walk by are wrecked or abandoned with the doors open. There's blood everywhere. I consider stealing one of the cars, but I don't need any more dead on my trail, no more than the single guy from the woods who's been following me and slowly succumbing to his wounds. His pulse slows and slows and... slows. It's going to stop completely soon. And I really don't want to be around him when it does.

I can smell something familiar in the air. Someone was here. Sparrow was here. I follow the smell of him and thank my lucky stars that those runes didn't take away his scent.

I follow the trail to an empty house. Around back, I kick open the door and let myself in. The place is a dump with holes in the floor and filled with dust. He was here. I walk through the kitchen and find a couch with blankets. He slept here. There are footprints on the floor, a fresh indent in the couch. I take my time looking around to see if he left anything. Sparrow's not in his right mind and might've left something behind. It's a lie I tell myself. Even when he was the most cracked in the head, he never left anything behind.

I sit in the indent on the couch. The back door of the house creaks. I wait. Maybe it's him? Could it really be this easy? A figure lumbers through the door and crashes into the kitchen chairs. Damn. It's my dead friend from the highway.

Gripping my blade, I step aside and give him room to schlep on over.

"I told you to stay away from me." I'm not sure why I'm bothering to talk to the walking bag of flesh.

Jaws snap.

These dead are nothing like the ones down in Hell. At least down there they give me space.

I brace myself for the lurch that comes next. Sidestepping, I swing my arm out and cut off the dead man's head. His body drops to the ground. I walk toward the kitchen and get my bearings.

I leave the house without any more clues about Sparrow. I follow his scent mixed with the sea salt spray of the nearby Pacific ocean. It's not a scent of Hell. No, this is something different. Danger and freshness and energy linger around the smell of him. I follow the empty streets. The dead are upright here, meandering and moaning, but they keep their distance for now.

I stop at a bar near the town limits. The neon lights still blink in the window. Why would Sparrow go to a bar? I can only think of one reason. He was hungry. A shiver runs up my spine and my arms tingle. The thought of Sparrow seeking out blood from another woman... I know better. Skeele warned me. I don't go into the bar. I don't want to know the details. I don't want to see the corpses. I turn to the right and follow the road out of town.

The sign points to Redwood highway again. North. I notice a

lump of something on the ground. As I get closer, I recognize the dead crow. I touch it with my toe and notice it's missing two flight feathers. If I had anyone to bet money with, I'd bet those two feathers are in Sparrow's pocket right now. I'd rather it was me.

I stop at a small house just past the edge of town. The day didn't last long and as the sun started to set, the noises in the woods started. Now, I'm a creature of Hell, but I still have fear of the horrors of the Earthen plane. I lived through enough of them growing up. I'll catch up to Sparrow eventually. I'll take my time; don't want to roll up on him like some crazy ex-girlfriend and scare him off. Who knows what his mental state is like right now. I need to be careful because I need to take him back with me.

FEATHERED FRIENDS BRING GIFTS

SPARROW

Sparrow is a shadow in the night, a pale giant in the morning light. Shay and Jed have been waiting for him. Every few miles he walks, there they are, waiting. Expecting. Watching. Anticipating for a sign. Waiting for him to show them what he really is.

"You might want to hurry up," Shay says, tucking blue hair behind her ear. "Something is following us."

"It's me," Sparrow says.

"No," Jed finally speaks up. "Something worse than you. Something darker than you." He raises his forearm and the runes tattooed there glow blue. "They aren't supposed to find us." Jed's forehead wrinkles.

Sparrow blinks and then holds up his arms. His runes are dark. There's no blue glow. Just an ethereal iridescence.

"They were supposed to hide us," Jed says.

"We need more weapons," Shay says.

"So, who is it?" Sparrow asks.

"We aren't sure," Shay says. "But if we have any chance of surviving, it's with you."

"We know each other?" Sparrow asks.

"Yes," Jed says. "We've met twice in this lifetime. And each time our paths cross, chaos follows."

A shadow passes over them before landing behind Sparrow. Another follows. Then another.

They're crows. One drops a stick. Another drops a pocket knife. The third drops a small handgun.

"Don't touch it," Shay warns.

Sparrow kicks it away. "Don't need it."

Shay bends and picks up the gun, inspecting it. "Smart birds. I've never seen them drop something like this from the sky though."

Sparrow picks up the knife and tucks it in his pocket.

Unbroken Curses

I peek out the cracked window as the sun starts to rise. It's been three days. I'm out of time. The solstice is over. Heaven and Hell will be looking for me. That's okay. I've seen enough Jason Bourne movies to know what to do. I trace the runes on my arms. They're supposed to hide me, like Sparrow's do. I'm hoping it will take very long for someone to recognize me.

I toss the dusty blanket off me onto the floor and stretch. Sleeping in a chair wasn't the best idea but I couldn't bring myself to sleep in someone else's bed. Never could. I'd flipped all the pictures down in the room before falling asleep, unable to tolerate the stares from the people who lived here before. I wonder if they're dead now. I wonder if they packed their shit and ran to Canada with the hopes that the walking corpses would freeze in the snow, and they'd be safe from death by zombie bite?

I shrug in self contemplation. Sounds like a good idea. I'm sure someone has thought of it.

I reach for my bag and grab two of the protein bars Noah

packed for me. The canteen is nearly empty, just enough to rinse my mouth out from the chalky taste. My stomach growls.

"Yeah. Yeah." I tell myself. "We'll find more food." I zip up my bag and sling it over my shoulder as I get a hard look at the street. From the second story, everything looks empty and quiet. What would Andy Dufresne do? I escaped. He escaped. I dream for a moment about sunny beaches and swaying palm trees, about treasure and white speed boats...

A loud clang from downstairs startles me. Crap. The place looked empty last night and I didn't notice anyone alive or dead when I walked through. Maybe they came in while I was asleep? I glance out the second-story window again. Wings would help right now. I could just fly away and avoid whatever shit-fuckery is going on downstairs.

There are slow footsteps, shuffling, furniture falling over and grunts.

I step toward the stairs and see shadows in the early morning light. I tighten my bag and grip my blade, ready. I walk down the steps slowly, staying near the wall. There's less of a chance of them creaking near the wall. I walk down a few more until I can see figures in a far mirror along the wall. The dead got in. And so did someone else.

I glance at the front door at the bottom of the stairs. I could run down and out. Or go back up and out a window and hope I don't break a leg jumping down. I catch a glimpse of blonde hair escape from under the cloak.

Wait a minute...

I run down the stairs to get a closer look.

One of the dead notices me and staggers closer. They're coming in through the back door, one after another. I take a few steps forward and chop off its head.

The person in the cloak turns at the sound, the hood falling back.

"Teari?" I ask.

She slices two heads off and backs up, kicking over a chair to block the deads path.

"I was trying to sneak up on you," Teari says.

"You failed at that," I say backing toward the front door.

"Your father sent me. You were supposed to be gone by morning." Teari moves toward me, unlocks the front door and opens it.

She pauses. "Bangs?"

I push my hair out of my eyes. "Shut up."

"Let's get out of here." She tips her head at the doorway.

She doesn't have to ask me twice. We run through the door and slam it closed.

As soon as we clear the house that's under siege, I ask, "How on God's green earth did you find me so fast?"

Teari smiles. "Being a healer, I have gifts of my own." She wags a finger. "You should know better than to think you could hide from me."

We jog down the street, ducking behind cars to catch our breath. The morning fog is thick.

"I think we've lost them," I say.

Teari nods in agreement. "So, where are we headed?"

"You're not going back, now that you found me being bad on the Earthen plane?"

"Nope," Teari smiles. "Go back and let you have all the fun? No way." She stands and stretches. "I'm guessing you're walking. You always walk. Which direction?"

I point toward the highway. "That way."

We scan the town and make sure none of the dead are following.

We walk the highway as the sun clears the sea mist.

Teari moves toward the edge of the road. "You think this was him?" she nudges a dead raven.

"Are there feathers missing?" I ask. "If there are, he was here."

Teari crouches down to inspect the bird. "Yup. Flight feathers are gone."

"Figures."

We walk US-101 north. There are signs for campgrounds and the Redwood forest. Teari nods toward the campground sign. "Guaranteed trouble there."

"I avoided the trouble at the last one."

"Speaking of trouble," Teari says. "Have you seen baby Thrush lately? Poor Nightingale never gets much sleep anymore. She always looks completely exhausted. I guess a baby will do that. Soon he'll be walking and tearing the place up." Teari smiles, thinking about Sparrow's nephew. "Oh sorry. I'm sure she hasn't brought him to see your realm. You'll spend lots of time with him when he's older."

"Why's that?" I ask.

Teari pauses before saying, "He's cursed just like the rest of them. He'll spend his time as a Hellion eventually."

Crap.

Friends of a Feather

Shay waited at the exit to Elk Valley Cross Rd. She turned off the Jeep to save gas and propped her feet up on the dashboard.

"He walks pretty fast," Jed said, digging in his backpack for something to eat.

"Then we shouldn't have to wait long." Shay shivered. She didn't like to be a sitting duck on the highway. The only solace was that Sparrow would be there soon and he'd scare away anything threatening.

"Why didn't you just ask him to ride?" Shay asked Jed.

Jed chuckled. "Not so sure I want to be sitting in the same vehicle as him. Last time I was in the same room as Sparrow, his girlfriend nearly killed me. I have little trust for creatures of Heaven and Hell combined."

Shay nodded. "Understandable."

A few of the dead ambled by. Shay and Jed held their breath and sat still as stone until they passed.

"I haven't seen them move ahead of Sparrow before," Shay whispered.

Jed nodded in agreement. "There must be something going on up ahead drawing them."

It was just a few hours until Sparrow caught up with them. Shay rolled down the window as he headed toward the exit to Elk Valley Cross Rd. "Where you headed, Sparrow?" Jed asked.

He didn't answer. Shay followed, her foot barely pressing the gas pedal.

They followed him past Sunset High School and turned right on Lake Earl Drive. They passed a pub and a T-shirt shop before Sparrow turned left onto Buzzini Road.

Shay and Jed saw what drew Sparrow. There was a giant house in front of them set on a lake and surrounded by a stone wall. Music thumped from inside.

Shay and Jed made eye contact. They'd seen what he did to the bar in Crescent City.

"We have to shut this down," Shay said.

Jed shook his head and made a face. "We aren't the police. What those people are doing is a death sentence."

Shay kept driving, looking for a parking spot that was both hidden but close. "They're probably just stupid kids." She thumbed to the road behind them. "Did you see the high school we passed?"

Jed leaned forward to open his bag and take out weapons. "Just so you are aware, I am not a fan of this."

Shay found a spot under the overhang of a large tree and near the stone wall that surrounded the mansion. They could get in and out easily and avoid most of the zombies that were currently knocking on the gate.

Sparrow walked up to the house, around the horde, and jumped up on the stone wall. He watched the house for a few minutes. The music pulsing wasn't much different from the pulsing of blood through veins.

He jumped down and walked toward the front door of the house. It was unlocked. He let himself in.

More Dumb Ways to Die

At the end of the world there are always parties. The young people never fail in that aspect. I started off by following Sparrow's scent. It let me to a gated mansion near a lake.

The dead are clawing against the brick wall and leaning into the thick, iron gate. It must be cheap iron since it bends under their weight. Or maybe they've been pining for what's inside for some time now.

I used to do a lot of dumb things, but I don't think I was ever dumb enough to throw a rager in the middle of the zombie apocalypse.

A night breeze rustles the dead leaves on a nearby tree. It brings the pungent smell of the dead. I gag a little and cover my mouth.

Teari's head snaps in my direction and she holds a finger to her lips, effectively telling me to swallow the puke and not cause a scene. I pull my shirt over my nose and take a few breaths. When the breeze stops, I let it fall back into place. Teari walks closer, blade in hand. Ready.

I can smell him. Faintly. He could be here.

Teari makes a questioning face and tips her head in expectation.

I nod.

Teari walks away and surveys the place. I notice a few trees and consider climbing one and jumping across the brick wall into the yard.

"Are you sure he's here?" Teari asks.

"Yes."

"How do you know? I have no sense of him anymore," Teari says.

"I can smell him."

"Like his cologne?" Teari asks.

"Like his blood," I reply.

"Oh." Teari reaches for her blade. "I could carry you over the wall."

"No." I shake my head. "That's too humiliating."

"Why do you never take the help that's offered?" she asks.

"I don't want to owe you anything," I say.

"I don't keep a tally."

I can't hide my expression of surprised disbelief. "Everyone keeps a tally," I say. "Everyone."

"Do you?" Teari asks.

"Of course."

"Then what do I owe you?"

I press my lips together, holding it in.

"Tell me." She urges.

"There was that one time when I was stabbed, and we were trying to escape, and you told Sparrow I wasn't worth the risk."

"And I owe you something for that?" She paces and watches the crowd of the dead. Teari is full of arrogant pride. She's always been that way. Can't hate on her for it.

"An apology," I say.

Teari sighs before turning to face me directly and saying, "I'm sorry. You were worth the risk."

"Thanks." I step to the side. "I think I'm going to climb that tree and drop down." I point to the giant oak tree near the wall.

"Just let me help you."

"No." I hold up my hand to stop her. "You can't be flashing around all your glory." I circle my hands around her. "It will bring questions." I tighten my bag and run for the tree. "The few left alive could see. They'll be spreading your image in newspapers and what news channels and social media platforms are still up and running."

"I just don't want us to fuck this up." Teari rests her hands on her hips. "There's enough turmoil in the Seven Kingdoms of Heaven that I must go back to. If I don't help you fix this, who knows what they'll blame on me."

"Are they threatening you?" I step toward her, raising my voice. It's hard not to. You see, I have this problem with wanting to put jerks in their place. Especially righteous jerks from Heaven. They've caused Sparrow's family enough grief. "Did they?" I ask again, louder.

Oops. Too loud. The dead notice us.

"Run," Teari takes to the air.

I race the dead to the tree trunk. I run and focus on a low branch. The dead start moving toward me. I dash the last few feet, jump, and grab the lowest branch to pull myself up. As my feet dangle, one of the walking sacks of flesh grabs at my boot.

"Get up there, Meg," Teari shouts from above me.

I pull my body up then climb to standing. I secure my foot in the vee of the trunk and climb up a few large branches. "You cheat," I say, out of breath.

She climbs down, balances on the branch that stretches over the wall, walks it like a circus girl on a tightrope, and jumps down.

I follow her, although I'm not as graceful, stopping to secure my bag in one of the vee's of the tree trunk. I don't want to bring a backpack to a party. Those kids will probably be looking to score anything for a high. I know I did at their age.

I drop to the ground and roll before moving back to my feet. "See?" I say. "Easy."

"Uh-huh." She's staring at the mansion. "Should we just march in the front door?"

"Why not?" I shrug. "It's the apocalypse as far as these people know. Locks don't matter anymore."

"Hopefully not for much longer."

I skip to keep up with Teari's long stride as she heads for the door. The metal driveway gates clang behind us. I turn to see the horde there, reaching, growling, teeth clanking. For the first time in my life, I wish I were back in Hell. At least there the dead stay away.

Teari raises her hand to knock, but realizes the door is cracked open. She pushes it open further and we walk inside. The music is blaring classic rock. I smell beer and sweat and sex. I follow the noise, walking away from Teari. She's an adult and can handle herself. I've got one thing on my mind and that's to find Sparrow.

There are people on couches, eating at the giant dinner table, and sitting on the floor on pillows. They barely notice me, probably due to their inebriation. I'd love to be inebriated right now. I cross the threshold into a huge open living room. All the furniture is gone, there's a DJ booth set up in front of the wall of windows that leads to a pool area. The room is packed and everyone is dancing.

I search the crowd for a millisecond before I find who I'm looking for; the tall, dark-haired man in the center of the room.

Sweet goddamn. He's surrounded by a bunch of hussies all rubbing up on him and shit. Oh Hell no. I enter the crowd and dance my way to the center. There's lots of groping, lots of stares. Sparrow pauses when he sees me. I get closer and nudge a blonde out of the way.

Ah, there he is. My Sparrow. Tall, dark. So dark. I don't ever remember him being like this. Shadows grace the hallows of his face and neck. There is some type of energy surrounding him. It's intoxicating.

"You..." He whispers.

"You," I reply. "I've come a long way to find you."

Another blonde chick starts rubbing up on him. I shove her away with a one-armed thrust to the side.

"Hey!" the chick shouts.

I hiss at her. "Fuck off."

Sparrow touches my shoulder. He's dancing, slender hips moving with the heavy beat of the music.

It's been too long since he last touched me. Sparrow moves his leg between mine and starts dancing like we are in a dirty movie. Classic Meg and Sparrow. If I allow this to go on for one more second, one more heartbeat, there's no going back. This feels too good. I give up, give in, let the darkness consume me and touch him. Oh...

Sweat drips down my spine. His hands are touching my body. Touching me in places where there's ink hidden under my clothes.

"Why are we like this?" he asks. "Who are you?" He tips his head, birdlike and perfectly Sparrow. I wait for him to whistle a trill that never comes.

I spin and grind against him. Sparrow's large hands are on my shoulders, they slide down my arms to my hips. I press harder against his crotch.

He groans.

"Yes." I press my head to his chest and grind harder.

His hands slide under my top and across my stomach. I spin to face him.

"Who are you?" he repeats.

"You don't remember me?" I ask. The old Meg would be pissed. She'd kick him in the crotch and cross the dance floor to find someone else. Not the Meg I am now. He's mine. I'm his. He'll remember soon enough. I'll make him remember.

I reach up, my hands sliding across his chest, his shoulders, his neck. I stop and feel the steady pulse there. His eyes look different.

"You don't remember me, Sparrow. But I remember you. I crave you."

The music pulses. He glances down the wide neck of my shirt and notices the watercolor tattoo of a sparrow in flight.

"I like that," he says.

"I know you do. There's more." I lift the hem of my shirt as I dance and move in a tight circle.

Someone growls.

I spin to look at Sparrow.

He's searching the room.

"That wasn't you?" I ask.

"No," he replies.

There are screams from the corner of the room. Bodies start shoving back. A few revelers trip and fall.

Teari walks into the room. I catch her gaze and point to the corner where the growling came from. She looks to me and slides her finger across her throat.

Crap. Someone died and my guess is now they're biting.

"Get him out," Teari shouts over the crowd.

The music stops suddenly and screams start near the corner of the room where Teari pointed. Oh no. Shit is about to get real.

"Come with me," I say as I grab onto Sparrow's shirt and tug. He doesn't move. "Come on!"

"I'm hungry," he mutters, his eyes on the panicking people who are shoving their way out the doors.

"I'll feed you. Come with me, Sparrow. Now!"

Sparrow's head twists quick as his eyes settle on mine. "Feed me?"

"Yes." I tug harder at his shirt until he starts moving. "Come with me now." I lead him toward the slider doors to the pool. There's a bottleneck of people trying to get out. I shove my way through. Sparrow's stronger, he shoves harder. Dude must be starving.

We get out the door and break free from the crowd. I grip his hand and run toward the side of the house. I need to get back to the tree where I left my bag. And I need to find Teari.

"Teari!" I shout as we round the side of the house. "Meet us at the tree!" I don't know where she is, so I shout blindly.

We round the side yard only to be met with the horde.

"Shit," I mutter, gripping my blade and pulling it off my leg.

Sparrow makes a growling sound. A few of the dead back off but a handful make their way toward us. I put my blade to work, heads roll. It's been a while since I've had to use it. Feels kinda good.

"You're not going to help?" I ask Sparrow.

He has his blade ready. They're both glowing. I'm sure we're breaking a heck of a lot of rules between realms right now, but this is life or death. And there's no way I'm going out by being bitten by a dead thing.

We slice, dice, and run for it. I shout to Sparrow to head toward the tree. Thankfully he obeys.

"Meg?" Teari yells from the backyard.

"The tree!" I shout back.

Teari runs, leaps and —something grabs her. Gray arms tug at her. She screams and struggles until she finds her weapon and frees herself by hacking wildly, then launches herself into the air again.

I dash for the tree. Sparrow follows. So do the dead. They move faster than I remember. Their speed is like a bad dream. Maybe it's the drugs from the party?

"Help me reach," I say, motioning to Sparrow. He lifts me and tosses me up like I weigh nothing. I grab a branch and swing my leg over the side, straddling it. "Come up." I motion for Sparrow to follow. He assesses the brick wall and backs up. The dead are getting closer. Too close. Sparrow runs a few steps and leaps to the top of the wall but one of the dead grab his leg, then another, and another. He groans as they tug, jaws snapping.

"No!" I scream. This isn't supposed to happen. How could this happen? "Teari!" I shout.

I glance back. Teari is on her way, flying at warp speed. She's going to slam into us.

"Slow down!" I shout.

She's gripping her injured arm, her blade glowing in her opposite hand. She lands shakily on the top of the wall next to Sparrow. She grabs his arm and pulls him up the wall. Sparrow kicks off the dead and stands, gripping a branch above his head to steady himself.

"What the fuck just happened?" I ask.

Teari holds up her hand and I notice the rotting teeth marks. Blood drips out of the wound and down to her elbow in dark red rivulets.

"Oh no," I say.

Blackness starts going up her arm, following the outline of her veins.

"Can you heal yourself?" I ask.

Teari's a healer, that's what she's always done; used her angel magic to heal me and others.

"I've never tried on something like this," Teari says as she closes her eyes and holds her uninjured hand over the wound. She shakes her head, defeated. "I can't."

"You have to," I urge.

"It won't work on this," she says, giving up. "Do you have an extra shirt?"

"Yeah." I move to standing on the giant branch and wobble to my bag that's stuck in the vee of the tree. I never thought to bring a med kit. I unzip the bag and pull out my spare T-shirt.

Teari moves closer to me. "Are you ready?" Sweat is dripping down her perfect face.

"For what?"

In a quick movement she holds out her injured arm and slices it off above the elbow with her blade.

"What in the hell?" I scream.

"Wrap it!" Teari shouts back. "Don't let me bleed out! Hurry up!"

Blood is spurting out, drawing the dead closer to us. They collect along the brick wall. I look to Sparrow. His eyes are on blood. I've seen that look before.

"Can't you stop it?" I ask.

"You know how you can't poof when you're injured? Similar thing here. Too much energy being used. Forget about my healing powers, we're running on pure science and bog witchcraft until this heals."

"Well this sucks." My fingers fumble with wrapping her stump. My stomach growls. I pause to focus and control the bloodlust.

"Wrap it tighter!" Teari shouts. "You must stop the bleeding. You have to squeeze the arteries."

I wrap my T-shirt around the remaining half of her arm and stretch it, tying the sleeves. Blood soaks through and drips down the wall.

The dead scramble, licking the bricks and rubbing their faces on it.

"Umm..." a strange thought crosses my mind, probably from too many horror movies and supernatural TV shows. "Teari, what is your blood going to do to them?"

"Huh?" she asks. She's looking really pale.

"Your angel blood," I specify. "What does angel blood do to walking corpses on the Earthen plane?"

"Never had the pleasure of coming across that problem," she mutters, her voice weak. "Do you think you could fly us out of here?" Teari asks.

"I can't fly," I say.

Teari makes a face.

We both look at Sparrow. He's watching the dead corpses lick the bricks. I scan the trickles of blood and notice one coming from under his boot.

Shit. Shit. Shit.

I move across the wall, steadying myself by gripping a tree branch overhead.

I bend down and pull up Sparrow's pant leg. There's a large chunk of flesh missing and blood streaming down his leg.

I want to puke. I want to *poof* the fuck back to Hell so I can be safe in my little castle with my group of Hellions to protect me.

"What's wrong?" Teari asks.

We've been in some whacked out situations, but this is by far the worst.

"He's bit," I say.

"Cut it off," Teari says. "Cut off the bitten limb."

"It's his leg!" I shout. "You want me to cut his leg off?"

"Yes!" Teari screams back at me. "Get us the hell out of here or cut his leg off!" She leans into the tree, breathing heavy.

Sparrow growls. "You will not cut off my leg," he says.

"What did he say?" Teari asks.

"He said I can't cut off his fucking leg," I reply. "So what would you like me to do now?"

"Get us out of here, Meg!" Teari says.

Bird on a Wire

More of the dead cluster around the wall, shoving to lick the blood off the bricks.

"Now, Meg!" Teari holds out her stump of an arm, fresh blood dripping.

Jesus Christ. I can't fly them. We can't run. I scan the roads and nearby houses. I can *poof*. I look at Sparrow and Teari. I've never tried it with two in tow.

I have to try something.

I reach for Teari's hand and grip it tight. Then Sparrow's. I close my eyes and–*poof*–I bring them back to the Roman Catholic church in Pennsylvania where I first landed.

"Snow?" Teari scoffs and shudders.

"It's all I could think of," I say.

Fresh blood drips from Teari's stump.

Sparrow turns in a circle, palms out, catching snowflakes in his hands like a child. He leaves bloody footprints in the fresh powder.

I point to the front doors of the church. "Sanctuary?" I offer.

"Sanctuary from the cold and nothing else." Teari starts

climbing the stairs to the front door. "Can you even enter here?" she asks me.

There was a time when my daddy told me I'd burn to a cinder if I ever stepped foot in a church. I never have. But now… things are different. I'm different. I'm also cold. It's worth the risk.

I climb the steps. "We'll see what happens." I wave my arm. "Come on, Sparrow. Let's get moving."

Teari gets to the front door first. She presses on the handle and shoves hard. The door opens. She stops for a moment and listens.

Silence greets our ears. We stumble inside and close the door, sealing out the cold and snowy weather.

I pause for a second, waiting to feel myself go up in flames. It never comes. "I guess I can enter," I say.

"At least one thing can go right on this mission," Teari says as she walks toward the middle isle of the church.

Tall windows at the altar and toward the ceilings provide ample light for us to see. I wait and let Teari bait anything out of the rows of pews.

Sparrow is staring at my neck and making growling noises.

"Don't," Teari warns from the distance.

"Why?" I ask.

There's nothing I'd love more in this world right now than feeding off each other. It's been a long time since I've felt Sparrow's teeth on my neck. A long time since I've done the same to him. There's a wanting throb in my lower abdomen after dancing with him and being close. It took me so long to get him back again.

"Because you didn't cut off his damn leg." Teari points to Sparrow's bloody boot. "You want to turn into a walking corpse?"

Not really. For the first time in my life, I rather like my status. Turning into a walking corpse would really fuck that right up. So, no. I prefer not to turn into a walking corpse.

"Is he going to turn?" I ask.

Teari shrugs. "Probably. Nightingale is going to be pissed."

"Shit." I mutter. I don't want to feel Nightingale's rage.

"Not just Nightingale either," Teari warns. "All of Heaven is going to rain down their wrath upon us."

"We didn't do this," I remind her.

"We didn't prevent it." Teari touches the hilt of her blade as she stares at Sparrow's leg.

"Can't you heal him?" I ask. "You've healed us before."

"I don't know." Teari rubs her hand on her pantleg and makes a pained face. "I've never tried with something like this before. It could go terribly wrong." She presses her lips together in thought. "I don't trust myself to mess with it. Not like this." She moves her nub arm. "But, I can't even heal myself right now. I need to rest."

I step closer. "Sleep? Now? I don't think that's a good idea. We need to get the frick out of dodge."

"Now is not the time," Teari warns as she sits in the nearest pew. "I must rest. I've lost too much blood."

She does look considerably pale. Paler than I've ever seen her. She's always been tall and strong but right now she looks feeble and weak.

"Okay," I give in. "Okay, you rest." I glance to Sparrow.

"Don't you two do anything with each other," Teari warns.

I nod to myself and scan the room. The portal from Hell kicked me out here. I wonder if there's a portal back. Or maybe I could just poof between realms. Does it even matter if the other planes can tell I've left Hell? The balance is broken, fractured. God must be pissed. Not that I've cared much about how he feels. I glance around the church looking for anything obscure or out of place or glowing.

"Where are my friends?" Sparrow asks.

"What friends?" In all the time I've known Sparrow, he's never mentioned friends before.

"The girl with the blue hair and the tattoo guy." Sparrow motions to the tattoos on his arms.

There's only one tattoo guy.

"Jed?" I ask.

Sparrow nods.

Of all the fucks I've come across. I can't wait to find him and knock some sense into him for covering Sparrow in runes.

"Who is the girl with blue hair?" I ask, trying not to sound jealous.

He shrugs.

"Where did you leave them?" I ask.

"At the party," Sparrow replies.

"They're probably dead now," I say.

We barely made it out alive. And only time will tell how alive we really are by morning.

"I need them," Sparrow says.

"Why?" I ask.

"They need us," he replies. "There's no one else for them." He waves in the direction of California. "They don't belong out there."

Jed is from central New York, I doubt he has much to go back to. His shop was nearly ruined last time we were there, and he told me he's spent his life on the run because he doesn't belong. He's a hybrid and he's been hunted since childhood. Always hiding. Always on the run. He knows spells and magic I've never come across before. Maybe I shouldn't hate on Jed too much.

"I'll go get them," Sparrow says as he moves toward the door.

I grab his sleeve to stop him. "No. I'll go."

Poof. I return to the stone wall.

The dead still lick at the blood, they've almost cleaned the stone. I crouch and think of a game plan. I don't want to wander around on foot searching, I want to get back to the church ASAP. I have to find Jed and this other woman.

The daylight is starting to takeover. I squint and focus on the windows of the mansion where the rave was held. Survivors are rare after a shit show like that. If I were trapped inside, I'd go up. I've done it before and survived. I watch the windows, scanning them for movement. Poof. I flash to the porch overhang, getting my footing on the pitch. I look in the windows. The first one is a hallway of the dead. I ease away from that window, hoping they didn't see me. The next is an empty bathroom. The next is a room with the door barricaded shut. I crouch and watch. After a few moments I notice the barrel of a handgun pointing out of the closet door. Shit.

Bang!

I duck to the side as the bullet breaks glass.

The noise calls the dead. The ones from the hall start pushing on the window. I peer through broken glass, and the barricade is heaving. *Poof.* I flash inside to the closet door and kick it open. It's Jed and a woman with blue hair.

"Jed, nice to see you again," I say as I motion for them to come with me. "Would you like to get the fuck out of here?"

The chick nods and picks up a bag off the floor. I hold out my hands. "Let's go."

It wasn't so long ago that I despised being touched. This is different.

Jed looks at the chick and nods.

They both grip my hands.

We *poof* into the church where I left Teari and Sparrow. Jed turns to the side and vomits.

"Sorry," Jed mutters as he wipes his mouth on his sleeve.

Shay makes a face of disgust.

There's a strange gurgling sound that echoes throughout the church.

"Sparrow?" I ask, looking around. I notice Sparrow hunched over the pew where I left Teari.

"Oh my god!" I shout. "Sparrow, no!" I run toward him, grab the back of his jacket, and tug him backward with all my strength.

When the Blood Runs Out

Meg

I glance down at the pew. Teari is still asleep but she has a new bite mark on her remaining hand.

"What in the holy fuck, Sparrow?" He snaps at me. Teeth snapping and eager. "Ah!" I shove him in the chest as hard as I can. He stumbles back and falls. That's strange. Either I gained some magnificent strength, or something is seriously wrong with him. Sparrow is nearly three times my size.

I take a closer look. He turned while I was gone. He's sickly and gray and his darkness is something different now.

I feel sick. Why can't I just have my Sparrow? Why is he always transitioning to something else? He's never been just Sparrow; always fluttering between planes and curses and duty. It changes him so drastically. Still, I know one day I'll finally see Sparrow without all of that, one day it will just be him. Until then, I've been enjoying the pieces of him that shine through. I'm not sure how much will shine through this version of Sparrow though. My father once told me, *time as a Hellion spares no Angel's original form or mindset*. Still, I never dreamt I'd see him as a walking dead man.

Teari moans. I turn and shake her awake.

"What's going on?" she mutters.

"Ah" how do you tell someone they've been bit? In their only remaining hand?

"Kill her!" Shay shouts, unsheathing a gun from her hip holster. "Kill her before she turns!"

My fingers hover over my blade.

"Who turns?" Teari asks as she rubs her face. Pauses. "What the…"

She sees it. The black marks in the shape of Sparrow's bite. Perfect black ovals embedded in her hand.

"No." Teari says with an exasperated whisper.

"Kill her now," Shay says.

I hold out a hand. "Stop."

Teari holds out her hand. "Cut it off. Now, Meg." She waves her hand as the black starts to spread. "Cut it off now!"

"You'll have no hands," I say.

"I don't care. Cut! Now!" she screams at me.

I grip my blade. It glows in the fading light. Teari holds out her arm. Whack. The bitten hand falls. Long, delicate fingers curling in on themselves. Her hands had healed so much.

"Wrap it," Teari reminds me.

Blood is pouring out of the fresh wound. I reach for my bag and pull out my last clean shirt. Never thought I only packed to bandage wounds with my clean clothes and never wear them.

Sparrow is growling and moving to his feet. Clumsy. I've never seen him clumsy before. Only limber and strong. Something is very wrong.

"Secure him," I order Shay and Jed. "But don't kill him."

"What are you going to do with a dead man?" Jed asks.

"Whatever the fuck I want," I reply as I wrap Teari's wound. I have to do something with him. I have to get him to safety so I can figure out how to fix him.

Cloth rips and as I'm tightening Teari's bandage, I catch a glimpse of Shay standing on the pew and wrapping fabric around Sparrow's lower face. Smart. Now he can't bite anyone else. Jed is wrestling with Sparrow's arms, doing his best to tie them behind his back.

"You should have cut his leg off. You're going to need to help them," Teari warns. "I'm going to pass out now."

Her head thumps against the wooden pew. I take in the sad figure. Teari was once formidable. A warrior, a healer. She went head-to-head with Hellions and my father and those asshole Archangels in Heaven. She doesn't deserve this.

Should I have cut his leg off? He told me not to. What would a one-legged Sparrow have gotten us? Getting him mobile with one leg would have been a bitch. He'd be starving after the blood loss. I swallow hard. He'd drain a whole town to fill himself again.

I scramble across the aisle, grab Sparrow's free arm, and twist it to meet the other arm that Jed is wrapping thin rope around.

"Where'd you get that?" I ask.

"Bugout bag," Shay replies. "Never unprepared. My parents trained me for times like this."

A memory of Jim taking me on long hikes pings to the forefront of my mind.

I scan her closer and notice the sneaker-like hiking boots, rip proof pants, and bracelet made of paracord. The girl has it all. I notice the bag on the floor is similar to mine with one shoulder strap that clips.

"Nice bag," I say.

Shay just stares at me.

I point at mine so she can see we have something in common. Well, something in common besides my boyfriend and tattoo parlor friend.

Shay nods in understanding. "What are you?" she asks.

Jed makes a noise as he struggles with Sparrow.

"Just let him go," Shay says to Jed. "He can't hurt anyone now. And he can't go far in this church."

I watch Sparrow meander down the aisle.

"Hey," Shay says to get my attention. "What are you?" she asks again.

"He didn't tell you?" I point to Sparrow.

"He never mentioned you," she says.

Ouch. I knew it, but it burns coming out of her mouth. "He didn't?" I ask pointing to Jed. "Jed and I go way back. He saved my ass a few times." I point to the tattoos on my arms. "Runed me up real good. Sparrow too."

"Nah," Shay shakes her head. "None of them mentioned you."

"Damn," I say, rubbing the spot over my heart. I hold out my hand to shake with her. "My name is Meg."

Shay doesn't move. Her eyes narrow on me. "You are something." She moves her hands in the air around me. "Dark. It's very dark around you. I don't trust you."

Jed elbows Shay.

"What?" Shay asks, annoyed. "You're just Meg?" she asks. "Nothing more than Meg?"

"She's much more," Jed warns, looking a bit more frightened of me than the last time we were standing in a room together.

"Look," I raise my hands. "Sparrow asked me to get his friends, so here we are. I didn't bring you both here for any other reason." I cross my arms over my chest. "But now I have a busted ass healer Angel and a zombie for a boyfriend." My stomach growls loudly. "And I'm hungry. So, we need to get the fuck out of dodge before Heaven sends some shitheads down here to screw things up more."

Jed makes a noise. "I knew that getting mixed up with you was going to send me on the run." He points, accusingly. "I told you that I can't trust anyone. Not even a girl who can flash between realms and slay the walking dead like she was born and bred to take of the apocalypse single handedly."

"You've said that before," I remind him.

"I repeated it to remind myself." He runs both hands through grown-out shaggy blonde hair.

Sparrow tasted Jed's blood last time we were together. He told me that Jed's is Nephelium of the Archangel Michael. He's been on the run his entire life.

"We need to get out of here," Jed says. "There's too many forbidden creatures in one room."

I nod in agreement. "I went through a portal that dropped me here." I start searching the room for anything resembling a portal or conduit to Hell. "Look for arches with inscription," I tell Jed and Shay. "I can't get everyone out of here at the same time."

We search the room. Every pew, every devotional space, every statue on display.

"There's nothing here," Jed says.

We meet at the altar. "I have to check on Teari," I say as I make my way back to the pew where she's resting.

Sparrow shuffles around the open space, knocking into things. His head tips to the side as he hears my footsteps.

Teari is ghost-white and blood drips from both her arms. Less than before but it's still enough to cause concern. My mouth waters. I clear my throat and focus. I know of a stone arch in a cemetery in Saratoga, but that is going to be hours away. I press my fingers to Teari's neck and feel a faint pulse. I bend and dip my finger in the pooling blood on the floor and touch it to my tongue. Damn. I grab the empty vial from my pocket, untwist the lid and scrape it through the pooled blood. Angel blood has got to help me. I don't know Teari's life story, but from what I just tasted, this could help me one day. I twist on the cap and shove the vial in my pocket as footsteps echo nearby.

Shay appears next to us. She grips the pew. "I read about this in a survival first aid book. I think it's shock."

"Oh yea?" I ask, trying my best to look nonchalant and not like I was just licking blood off the floor. "Angels can go into shock?"

"Why not?" Shay shoots back. "They're just giant supernatural offshoots of humans."

"Ok." I move hair off Teari's face. "What do we do?"

"Get the heck out of here," Jed warns. "I'm sure there's a car here somewhere. The priest would have needed to get groceries and travel."

"But did this priest hit the road when the dead started walking?" I ask. I glance at Sparrow. "How do we get him in a car?"

"Trunk," Shay blurts out.

The Scarecrow drove around with me in a trunk for a bit once. It wasn't fun rolling around back there. It did keep me contained. That's what we need to do with Sparrow. Contain him until we can fix him. I can't be cutting off any more hands today. I nod and begin collecting my things. "Let's find it."

The three of us head behind the altar to the elaborate door which leads to the priest's chambers. We search the office, every cupboard, every drawer, until Shay holds up a set of keys. "Score," she shouts. "A Cadillac."

"I hope it's got a big trunk space," I say.

Jed starts heading to a door at the back of the office. We follow him through a few hallways and out another door that leads to a garage.

"There we go," Jed says. "Every church like this has a similar layout." He unlocks the doors.

Shay searches the garage. "Keep your eyes open for gas cans or anything we can use."

"How far to the portal?" Jed asks.

I pull out my cellphone and load up Google maps. "It's almost a seven-hour drive," I say. "I'm not sure Teari is going to make it that far."

I show the screen to Jed. He nods. "I know how to get there from here." He makes a face. "You know, that's going to stop working soon. Surprised it's still got service."

Shrugging, I say, "Maybe I'm just lucky. You know how to get there?" I ask.

"I've been doing this a long time. Running, that is," he assures me as he starts the Cadillac and checks the gas gauge. "Well," he shouts over the engine, "someone wanted us to win today. There's a full tank."

"Good," Shay claps, "because there are no full gas cans here to fill the tank."

I reach for the garage door and pull up. We are greeted by the sound of shuffling feet and groaning.

"Crap!" Shay shouts.

I grab my blade and start chopping. There's about a dozen zombies looking to make us their dinner.

Shay lets off some head shots and I hold in the urge to tell her lay off the noise. Noise brings the dead.

Jed presses down on the gas and runs over the pieces of the corpses in the road.

My stomach sinks. No! He's frickin taking off. Now, I never did much to help him but what the heck?

Suddenly the brakes squeal and the window rolls down. "Meet me at the front steps," he shouts out the window before speeding to the end of the street and taking a sharp turn around the block.

"Come on!" Shay slaps my arm and heads inside.

We run through the hallways and offices until we reach the main area of the church again. I run down the steps of the altar, headed straight for Teari. Sparrow is shuffling near the back door like he knows what's up. Could he know what's up? Could Sparrow be in there and just unable to control the bloodlust since he's been infected with whatever it is these dead have? Wait. *It's just death*, I remind myself. They didn't change planes when they died. They're stuck here. It's just death. Nothing to be afraid of. We've died before.

"Help me lift her," I shout to Shay.

I grab Teari's shoulders. Shay grabs her legs and we shuffle her out of the pew and down the aisle of the nave. I walk backward as best as I can, arms burning. When I get to the door, I pause before kicking it open, hoping to knock over anything that might be lingering close and waiting for us. Hope surges as I see Jed rush out of the Cadillac and open the back door.

"Come on," he waves, "hurry up." He moves to the trunk and pops it open.

"I hope you could fit groceries from a trip to Sam's Club in there," I shout. "Sparrow's a big guy."

"He'll fit," Jed says.

I climb in the backseat and drag Teari in with me, resting her head on my lap. Shay bends Teari's knees until she can get the door closed.

I watch through the window as Shay and Jed run up the front steps of the church, open the door, and guide Sparrow out. He's able to walk down the steps. Sparrow grunts and groans and the rear of the Cadillac dips as he's settled in the trunk. I think... he must still be in there.

Shay and Jed slam the trunk closed and run to the front doors, each getting in. Jed shifts the Cadillac into gear and hits the gas.

I glance down at Teari's head resting on my lap. She's so still. I touch her cheek. It feels cool and she looks so pale. I check the pulse in her neck. It's faint. I move her arms and tighten the knots, trying to stop the flow.

My stomach growls. Being this close to fresh blood is going to be rough. The back of my seat moves as Sparrow knocks into it from the trunk. Seems the fresh blood is going to be tough on us both.

Jed drives like a bat out of Hell. He turns onto route 219, headed north. The cellphone in my pocket alerts us to turn around. I dig it out.

"This thing says we're going the wrong direction," I say.

"Nah," Jed says, accelerating. "We're going to avoid the busted down cars and roadblocks. I've been through these parts before. On my way to California."

"You drove to California?" I ask.

"There weren't planes flying when the dead started walking everywhere," Jed says. "They shut everything down."

"Sure weren't," Shay chirps in. "Driving was safest and fastest."

"Where did you two meet?" I ask.

There is a beat of silence as they glance at each other. Shay nods. "Nebraska," she says.

"You don't have to tell me," I say. I've been there. In that place where you don't want to tell anyone your life story and the terrible things that have happened to you. The way Shay tenses tells me a lot. Her walls are up. I'm not about to blast through them right now.

I brace myself as Jed turns right onto interstate 80. He passes two cars that are moving slowly. There's more broken down on the sides of the road. There's even some of the dead schlepping it down the highway. Jed weaves around them.

"Why'd you choose California?" I ask, settling my hand on Teari's chest. Feeling her faint heartbeat gives me an ounce of relief.

Jed clears his throat. "You know I've been on the run my whole life." He glances at me in the rearview mirror and in his reflection, I can see the blue aura that surrounded him the first time we met. Only in the reflection. "Months ago, the news stations were tracking the horde of dead. There were groupings of them all over the U.S. but the biggest one was in California." He clears his throat. "It moved strangely, stopping for days at a time before moving up the coast. I've been around long enough to know those things don't move in a coordinated pack like that. They're usually scattered."

I think for a moment, and he's right. Never once have I seen them moving as one giant group. Maybe little clusters here and there, but never a giant gathering.

"So, I had the thought that they must be following something... or, someone." Jed accelerates past three dead making their way across the highway. "I reached out to some of my contacts and they told me about the rumors of a tall, dark man walking his way up the coast. No one could tell what he was." Jed snaps his fingers and points into the rearview mirror at me. "But I knew. I knew because I never forgot the day you two showed up with Sparrow in that Canadian tuxedo."

"What's a Canadian tuxedo?" Shay asks.

Jed chuckles.

"Think jeans *and* a jean jacket," I say.

"Wow," Shay makes a face, "impressive. Wish I'd seen it."

"Nothing like it," Jed says as he slows to pass a family waving us down from their broken-down minivan. "Sorry," he mutters. "No room here."

"Keep going with the California story," I urge, settling my hand on Teari's chest to feel her heartbeat.

Jed clears his throat. "Once I started putting the pieces together, I headed that way."

"Why seek out Sparrow when you're trying to hide yourself?" I ask.

"Who better to hide with than a Hellion?" Jed asks. "I knew no one was finding him and the walking dead were keeping their distance. As far as I was concerned, being close to Sparrow was the safest option on the Earthen plane."

"It was," Shay says. "Most of the dead kept their distance when we got close to him."

After all the messed up things that have happened, at least a spec of good came out of it. Jed helped us, and Sparrow helped him. And he's helped me. Wait... why would he help me?

"Why have you stuck with me?" I ask.

Jed presses his lips together as he glances at me in the rearview mirror again.

"Why?" I urge.

"Because you're different than you were last time I saw you, Meg. You're stronger, darker, quicker. You've lost your spark." He tips his head. "What happened to you?"

I don't say a word. Didn't realize I was that easy to read. But I guess when you spend most of your life making bad decisions and killing Archangels, and stabbing your boyfriend in the heart to preserve the sanctity of the realms, I guess that changes you a bit.

"Whatever happened to you," Jed says, "is going to keep me safe. You owe me."

Damn. Jed plays a good game. I do owe him, a lot. Even though he pissed me off with that bullshit of tattooing Sparrow with runes of my blood to hide him from everyone, even me. It worked out though. I found him with other methods. And Jed has helped us. I haven't been out of the Earthen plane for long. Jed knows a lot more than I do about Archangels and demons.

"Shit," Shay blurts out and points. "Army men."

Jed pulses the breaks to slow the Cadillac and moves into the right lane. A row of Humvees blocks the highway. Men in green fatigues loaded with ammo and weapons are stationed at the roadblock.

"What is this?" I ask.

"Some kind of checkpoint," Jed says, rolling down his window.

"Just speed through them," I urge, my stomach twisting. "We can't stop."

"Nah," Jed says. "They'll shoot us dead." He rolls down all the windows and stops the car. "A caddy won't win against a Humvee."

Men in fatigues, carrying lots of guns and ammo surround us. "Where are you headed?" The one at the driver's side window asks.

"Saratoga Springs," Jed replies.

I hear the static of a walkie-talkie and footsteps nearing my window. My heart pounds in my chest. This is worse than when Raguel had me imprisoned in Heaven. At least there I had help with my father and Teari; there's no help here and there's nothing worse than a human man with weapons and an ego.

"We've got injured," a man shouts from my window. "Unlock the door," he orders. "Medic, medic, medic we need you at the on-ramp now," he hollers into his walkie-talkie.

"We have to get her home and get her help," I shout. "Just let us go!"

The locks click. My door is opened.

"Weapons, they've got weapons!" a soldier shouts from the other side of the car.

"Everyone has weapons you imbeciles!" Shay shouts.

The soldier that opened my door grabs my arm and drags me out. I fight. I slap and kick because that's what I do when manhandled on the Earthen plane; throwing punches or pulling out my blade would be a bad idea. "Don't touch me!" I scream. "We have to get her home and get her help."

"Why would you wait that long?" the soldier asks as he releases me and reaches for Teari's shoulders. Thankfully they don't seem to care much about our weapons. Maybe we look innocent enough. Maybe they've seen worse.

A whole crew of people show up and the soldier slides Teari on to a stretcher.

"What happened to her?" someone asks. I notice a red cross on the person's sleeve.

"She was bit." I motion to my hands. "She cut off one hand and then it happened again and she made me cut the other one off."

A medic checks Teari's pulse. "She's going to code soon," he shouts to the others. And then they are running her stretcher toward an ambulance.

"Wait!" I shout. "Don't take her away." I try to run toward the ambulance, but the soldier stops me.

"Let them do their work," he says.

I notice another soldier standing at the trunk. "What's in here?" he asks.

Jed is outside the car. He looks at me before saying. "Weapons for killing the zombies."

"And a little bit of food," Shay adds.

"You want to search it?" the soldier standing near the trunk asks the one in charge.

Shit. Shit. Shit. Shit. If they pop that trunk and find Sparrow in there, things will not be good. They're already not good and I didn't expect them to get worse. The small of my back breaks out in panic-sweat. I try not to act nervous. Damn it. If we'd just gotten to the portal we'd be home safe now and I wouldn't worry about being found.

The one in charge shakes his head. I guess he's got bigger fish to fry right now.

The soldier pats the trunk and points in the direction of the ambulance. "You can go wait for your friend while they fix her up."

We scramble into the Cadillac. Jed drives away, pulls off the Scranton exit and follows the signs to the hospital.

"That was close," Shay says.

"What are they going to do to Teari?" I ask.

Neither of them answer me.

A long time ago, Teari told Sparrow to leave me behind when I was injured. She didn't think I was worth it. I can't leave her on the Earthen plane, alone. I'm sure she'd do fine and eventually escape, but I just can't do it.

Jed parks in the hospital parking lot as close to the door as he can get. The place looks like a ghost town. Panic fills my chest. I've seen too many horror movies with fake hospitals and fake doctors.

Jed follows the signs for the emergency room and parks near the sidewalk.

"Go check on her," Jed says.

"And what about Sparrow?" I ask.

"We'll watch him," Jed says. "We'll be freezing our asses off in this weather while doing it."

I nod and get out. I jog toward the door, push it open, and make my way to the registration desk. The place is pretty empty. An old man sits on the far side of the waiting room. I stand at the desk. I hear voices in the back. I see a nurse running down the hall.

"Hey!" I shout. "I'm looking for my friend."

She ignores me.

"Hello," I say as I walk to the back.

No one responds. I follow the signs to the trauma bay. There are three medical staff working over the bed. I recognize Teari's long legs and pants.

"Hey," I say. "That's my friend."

No one replies, they're all too busy. I find a chair and move it to the open door of the trauma room. The medical staff move fast and shout technical jargon to each other like "tube her" and "Kelly clamps" and "another bolus" and "what the fuck is taking blood bank so long?". There's beeping from the monitors. This is like something from a war movie. I am taken back to a long time ago when I was brought into the ER, no longer pregnant and beaten half to death. I was in a coma. Teetering on the edge. But this isn't like what I experienced. The podunk hospital in Gouverneur had more resources than this place. At least they kept me alive. I'm not sure if this place is going to save her.

I sit in my chair and think of a game plan. We have Sparrow. And I have help. I'll have more help if I can get home. I glance out the window at the fading light. We are sitting ducks here. Someone is going to find us. I came here to find Sparrow and restore the balance, I remind myself. I don't need Teari for that.

I stand. "I'm going to come back for her," I say out loud.

"Sure," one of the nurses says as she hangs a bag of clear fluid on a pole. "It's going to be a while."

The staff don't seem to care much about me. But they are working their damndest to save Teari. That's all I could ask for. I show myself out.

A thin layer of snow coats the sidewalk and my boots leave footprints. Jed starts the car as I get closer. I get inside.

"How is she?" Shay asks.

I shrug. "No one could tell me."

Thuds come from the trunk.

"They'll help her," Jed says.

"We need to go" I start to say.

"And leave her here?" Shay asks.

I rub my face. "It's getting dark. We need to get to the portal. I have to get Sparrow to Hell before we're found."

"So we are leaving her?" Jed asks.

I say, "I'll come back for her."

Jed drives as fast as he can toward Saratoga Springs. I watch the shadowed forests from the window. We take I-84E and turn onto I-87N. Dark cities surround the Newburg and Albany exits. In the distance, there's lights. It seems some towns still have electricity. I try not to worry about how the Earthen plane will return to normal. They'll have to rebuild, bury the bodies after their souls leave, and put their world back together.

It's the early hours of the morning when Jed pulls into the stone driveway of the cemetery. I recognize the arch from when the Scarecrow brought me here.

Jed parks the caddy against the wrought iron fence. We get out and move to the trunk.

"I hope no one is watching," Shay mutters.

Jed pops the trunk.

Sparrow stares at us. I'm not a mind reader, but if I know anything about expressions, I'd say he's pissed. Although, if I were locked in a trunk for nearly eight hours, I'd be pissed too. Spending nearly one hour in a trunk made me want to punch Reuben in the throat.

"Come on, big guy," I say as I reach for his legs.

Getting Sparrow out of the trunk is a bitch.

We get him to his feet and guide him to the stone arch.

"To Heaven or Hell?" Jed asks.

"Hell," I reply.

He points to the words etched into the stone. "This can go to either."

"You can read that?" I ask.

He nods. "You can't?"

I can't fly and now I can't read. This moment ranks pretty high amongst the times I've felt inept.

"Tell me what they say." I point to the arch.

"Gradus ad infernus," Jed says and the space between the arch wavers. "Step to hell. That's it. Easy peasy."

I only know a little spell that Sparrow taught me before I knew who I was: "Angele Dei, illumina, custodi, rege et guberna." I glance at Sparrow. He was my guardian. Now, not so much. But the spell helped me travel before I learned to do it at will. I wonder what else it could do if I utter those words from my lips? Maybe they'd bring my father, King Gabriel. But then he'd be looking for Teari, and I don't want to answer that question.

I grab Sparrow's jacket at the elbow and help Shay lead him.

We step into Hell.

A Dark Welcome

Meg

We step into an open field. I know this place. I've been here before. My plane is just a dark reflection of the Earthen plane. We are a ways from Centralia, where my castle is nestled into the burning underground caves. *My castle*; it feels strange accepting it after all this time. Hi, my name's Meg. I killed Lucifer by sucking him dry of blood and now I live in a castle. Sounds impressive. Sounds a lot more intimidating than revealing I grew up in a trailer in the woods, raised by a demon whom I thought was my father... yeah, I think I'll stick with the first introduction.

"Where do we go now?" Shay asks.

I point south. "You know it as Centralia, PA."

Shay makes a sound of despair. "Are you kidding me? We just came from Pennsylvania." She runs her hands through the blow-torch blue hair and tugs at the ends.

"Seriously," Jed says, disgust in his voice. "Please tell me you have functioning vehicles down here."

"We do," I say. "But I didn't leave any nearby."

"You didn't plan very well," Shay says.

"Nope," I say. "Sure didn't. But no worries, someone will find us sooner or later."

Sparrow makes a noise but it's muffled from the cloth wrapped around the lower half of his face.

"Come on," I urge him. Sparrow walks better than I expected him to across the stone driveway and onto the paved street. We start walking down Green Ridge Road, our shoes echoing in the darkness. We turn left on Lincoln Ave and head for the intersection. Curtains move as the few souls who haven't found a Safe House hide out, waiting for their inevitable destiny of finding out they're dead. They'll wait for eternity, lost, if they don't find a Safe House soon. We turn left on Broadway, following the signs for the I-87 south.

"Weird," Jed says. "If I didn't know better, I'd say we already traveled these roads today."

"These are different," I say, then I change the subject. "Do you feel any safer, now that you're in Hell?" I ask Jed.

He shrugs. "All I can say, is I've never been here before. But those Angels have their ways."

"Not here," I say confidently. I have my crew of Hellions and demons and I can't forget my family of basilisks waiting in the castle for me. I shudder, remembering their slimy skin.

We pass a restaurant called The Sleepy Owl. "I miss diner food," Jed says.

"Same," I say. "What I wouldn't give for a large chocolate milkshake and some salty fries to dip in it." My mouth waters. I'll get it soon. As soon as Noah makes his appearance. Before I can call on him, the sound of footsteps break through the quiet.

"What's that?" Shay asks.

"Dead walking," I wave, dismissing it. "They'll keep their distance down here."

I take two more steps and the sound intensifies, moving faster. Wait. What's happening?

"Shit," Jed shouts. He grabs Shay's arm and tugs her away from the walking sack o' flesh that's currently running at us.

I grip my blade and glance at Sparrow.

There's a dead man headed straight for us at a pace I haven't seen since we were running from the drug infused party where I found Sparrow.

My blade glows, anticipating battle. I stand in the middle of the street, glancing toward the shadows to make sure there's only one. It gets closer, nearly running. I advance toward it, raise my blade, and chop off its head. The dead man drops to the ground. I kick its head away from the body. I've seen plenty of horror movies, don't want it reconnecting.

"Hm," I say as I secure my blade. "Haven't had that happen in a long time."

"What does that mean?" Jed asks.

"They usually keep their distance here." I search their faces. "Maybe it's because there's so many of us?" I suggest. "Come on, let's keep going."

We keep walking, quieter this time. And I have the urge to go back and drive the caddy through that portal. I don't think it's wide enough. I glance behind us. It's tempting. I want to poof back to the castle but I don't want to leave anyone behind for the second trip. Last time it didn't end well.

Twigs break and echo into the night as dead linger at the tree line like heifers in the shade.

It's not long before Noah appears in the road ahead of me. I missed his face.

"Noah, where have you been?" I ask.

He looks to Hellsky dreamily. "Birdwatching. You know how we used to do. Watching those songbirds all day long. What happened to it all?"

"We'll get back to it," I say.

Noah focuses on the group. "Oh! You brought back friends and..." he leans around me and notices Sparrow in the back. "What the fuck did you do to Sparrow?"

I grab Noah and something in me stills his ethereal form. "Do not tell Nightingale." I glance back at zombie-boy. "Actually, you are not to leave my presence until we figure this out."

Noah chuckles. "No soup for you."

My stomach growls on cue. "I'll have to eat something else."

"But, seriously, Night is going to be pissed. Beyond pissed, actually. You went back to fix things." Noah shakes his head. "This ain't fixing things."

"No shit, Sherlock." I point at the other two. "This is Jed. He's going to help us. And this is Shay."

"What's Shay going to do?" Noah asks.

"Something," I reply.

"Kick some ass," Shay says.

"I like her," Noah whispers in my direction. "Why aren't we going *poof* back to the castle?" Noah asks. "It would be faster than this method of travel."

"I can't take everyone at once. And I don't want to leave any of them waiting," I say. "Actually. Go get the Hellions. Tell them where we are."

"And leave your side?" Noah's lips tip up.

"Don't screw me over," I warn. "You've done enough of that."

Noah's eyebrows rise.

"Shut up," I warn. "Go get the Hellions. They can fly us back."

"Why don't you fly us back, Meg?" Noah asks, holding back laughter.

"You little...shit." I reach for his throat but Noah disappears into the darkness.

Jed and Shay are staring at me. I'm not revealing anything.

"Let's keep walking," I say. I lead the crew. Sparrow scrapes his feet behind me. I miss his singing and his feather obsession. His quirks made all our travels less boring.

"What are Hellions?" Shay asks.

"Giant, scary demon men," Jed replies.

"But you said Sparrow was a Hellion."

"He was. Or is. I'm not sure. Hey, Meg, what the heck is Sparrow these days?" Jed asks.

"Damned if I know," I mutter.

We walk further, passing the signs for the highway. I notice the asphalt is really crumbling along this road and I wonder if Hell has a department of public works.

"Oh my god," Shay shouts. "What the heck!" She grabs on to Jed, shielding herself with his body. "What are those?"

Skeele lands first. A wide smile that downturns almost instantly. "You took too long. We were worried."

I throw my hands in the air. "How about, great job, Meg? Or, way to go Meg? Or, look you found Sparrow, just what you needed to do," I scoff.

Heavy footfalls hit the pavement as the other Hellions land. Tukka, Chel, and Klaus look ready to fight and it takes a few moments for their tense poses to relax.

"Jed and Shay," I tell Skeele. "They're important to Sparrow." I glance behind Skeele. "Where is Noah?"

"He's at the castle," Skeele says.

A giant shadow covers us. Clea is here, in argentavis form.

Skeele gives orders. Chel carries Shay.

It takes two Hellions to carry Sparrow. Tukka grabs him from one side, Klaus from the opposite. They lift him into the sky, their bat-like wings strong and quick.

Skeele holds his arms out to me. "Wanna ride?" he asks.

I hesitate. Last time he had me in the sky he dropped me a few dozen times trying to get my wings out. I prefer not to subject myself to that again.

"Child," Clea calls, beckons.

"I'm going back with her," I say, thumbing towards the argentavis.

"Guess I'm taking the other guy," Skeele says as he moves toward Jed.

Clea lands. I run toward her and climb on her back. Clea spreads her giant wings, hops a few times and launches herself into the air.

In the distance I can see the Hellions flying and Sparrow dangling.

"Child?" she asks.

A mother knows.

"Everything is really fucked up," I say.

"There will be darkness and there will be light," her voice is soothing. "It never stays the same. Like the ouroboros, we are forever moving."

"I'm not sure I can fix this. Sparrow was bitten. He's something different now."

"He's always been something different," she says calmly. "Time will show you the answer."

I rub my fingers through her soft feathers and close my eyes as chilled air brushes across my cheeks. After all the running and fighting, the cool air feels good.

When we land at the castle only a few minutes behind the others, Noah is waiting, kicking pebbles around the dirt lot. He better not have told Nightingale already. He looks guilty.

"What happened?" Skeele asks, motioning to Sparrow.

"It was really bad," I say as I slide down Clea's side, my boots hitting the hard-packed red dirt. "Really bad."

"What happened to Sparrow?" Skeele asks.

"He was bit by one of the dead on the Earthen plane." I walk closer to Sparrow and motion to his boot. I don't tell them about Teari and thankfully neither Jed nor Shay mention her.

Sparrow groans, twists his neck like it's stiff, and flexes his jaws from under the mask Jed put on him.

"He needs to go somewhere safe until we can figure this out." I rub my face, exhausted and fed up. I want him to be in my room, but after what we just went through, I don't think that's a good idea. The only place I can think of that will keep him safe from harming others is locked up. "Put him in the dungeon," I say. "With eyes on him at all times."

"Meg…" Noah whispers, concerned.

"We'll figure it out," I say. "We have to." I head toward the door, Skeele close behind. "Give Jed and Shay rooms close to mine."

"Where are you going?" Skeele asks.

"To shower and change my clothes and think." I wave my hand. "Noah, come with me." I can't let him out of my sight again. I can't risk him going back to Nightingale and spilling the beans.

I open the giant wooden door that's built into the cave opening; woodsmoke and pine, it smells like home. Strange, I fought so long to find home. A place where I could be comfortable. A place where I felt I belonged. It took a while to sink in. I had to marinate here for a while. When the Deacons were drilling me for answers, they knew. They could tell I was searching for home, a home that filled my darkness, that cared for me, that sheltered me. I just didn't realize it back then. But, finally, this is home.

"Did you feed the basilisk babies and momma?" I ask Noah as I search the closet for something to wear, feeling squeaky clean not that I'm not covered in grime.

"Unfortunately," Noah replies, distracted. He's throwing birdseed over the balcony railing and songbirds are diving to catch the seeds. "Those things are nasty."

"I've been told they'll help us." I find a pair of dark jeans and pull them on.

"Help us, what?" Noah asks. "Help us despise walking into that office?" He makes gagging noises. "I want to puke every time I go in there to feed them."

I grab a black T-shirt and pull it over my head before leaving the closet and finding my bag. I find the small vial of Teari's blood and hide it in my nightstand drawer.

"You don't want anything to eat?" Noah asks. "It's been a while since I went to find pancakes or fried chicken or green eggs and ham."

"No thank you, Sam," I mock.

"Filled up on a little Sparrow while you were over there?" he asks.

"Nope. There wasn't time." I zip my bag and take it back to the closet for storage. "I would have liked too though."

I do wonder what it would do to me. If Teari chopped off her limbs, the result couldn't be pleasant. Maybe I'd turn into whatever Sparrow is now. Maybe it would put an end to all of these years of fighting to live.

I close the closet doors and glance out the window.

"You should eat," Noah urges.

"I can't risk you telling Nightingale," I reply.

"You're just going to starve?"

"Wouldn't be the first time."

Who Roams Here?

MEG

The conversation in the Hellion lair is interrupted by a bright flash of light. We shield our eyes. Skeele steps in front of me, a large hand pressing on my hip until I'm behind him, his other hand grips a wicked blade.

"Meg!" It's my father. He's covered in sweat and blood, his draped robes stained. He grips his blade, glistening with ichor. His knuckles are white.

The brightness of his arrival is swallowed by the darkness of the Hellion's lair.

"What are you doing here?" Skeele asks in a low grumble.

I push Skeele away to get a good look at my father. "What have you been doing?" I ask.

"Goddamn dead are roaming the Seven Kingdoms of Heaven." He secures his blade and the Hellions calm. "What did you do, Meg? You went to collect Sparrow to set it straight. Everything was supposed to go back to normal. Now we've got angels dying and that jackoff Raguel think's you've sent the dead as an act of war.

They're planning to punish you." Gabriel searches my face, waiting for a response. "And I can't find Teari."

I swallow hard. Those Angels love a good punishment. "I didn't do anything besides collect Sparrow and then we came back here as soon as we could."

"Where is he?" my father asks.

I wave as I head for the door. "Come with me."

Skeele's heavy footfalls follow as I open the door to the Hellion's lair and step into the hallway. My father barely looks out of place right now. He's usually bright, jovial even. Now, not so much.

Skeele leads us down long hallways, down cascading staircases chiseled from stone, past hallways and doors I have yet to explore. The smell of woodsmoke and pine and the heat intensifies.

"Don't look too closely," Skeele warns. "There are creatures down here that have been locked away for ages."

Gabriel grumbles something about "goddamned monsters."

We come to a large wooden door with a Hellion standing guard. There's a large square cut with metal bars. Skeele motions for my father to look.

Gabriel walks forward and peers in the window. "Jesus Christ." He turns to look at me. "What in the name of God happened?"

"He was bit by one of the dead," I say.

Gabriel rubs his face.

I don't elaborate.

"And where the Hell is Teari?" he booms. "We are being ambushed by those things. Have you seen them?" His eyes widen. "They run. They aren't like the ones down here, Meg. They're fast, they're different." He rubs his face. "We must figure this out. I need my healer. Where is she?"

"I don't know," I lie. "We lost her while we were running. It was a complete mess on the Earthen plane. The dead were everywhere."

"I told you to bring one of us," Skeele says.

I shake my head. "It wouldn't have helped."

"So you didn't send the dead to the Seven Kingdoms of Heaven?" Gabriel asks.

"No," I reply firmly. "I didn't send them. I would never. As much as I would like to show some of those jerks a taste of their own medicine..."

"I heard you've been having a problem with the Deacons," Gabriel says.

I turn to Skeele.

"They're under control," he promises. "We have them under control. Whatever this is, it is not the fault of this realm."

"If it's not you, and it's not the Deacons, then they are crossing the thresholds unassisted." Gabriel rubs his face. "What a goddamned mess."

A hissing sound interrupts our conversation. Sparrow is at the door opening, his face gray, his eyes sunken.

"Christ," Gabriel mutters. "How are you going to fix that?" he tips his head toward Sparrow.

"I don't know yet." I glance at Sparrow, longing for a version of him that's a little more alive, a little less flesh craving. "Somehow, we'll fix him. We always do."

Gabriel reaches for his blade.

Skeele pulls his own.

"Calm down, chuckles," Gabriel says. "I'm going back, and I have to go back ready to fight." Gabriel looks at me. "There are only two kingdoms who will believe you. Mine and Nightingale's. The odds are not good. The others will come for answers. They will want retribution."

"What are you telling me?" I ask.

"This is war." Gabriel's eyes widen as he focuses on me. And then he's gone, in a flash and speck of light.

.   .   .

"Have you been feeding Sparrow?" I ask Skeele and the other Hellion.

"We gave him food," Skeele says, crossing his arms over his chest.

"Did you give him blood?" I ask.

Skeele shakes his head. "What if it makes him too strong and he escapes?"

I lean against the door and take in Sparrow's side profile as he looks at the moon out the tiny window of his cell. Once he drank from me and inherited my ability to travel. Hunting him down again would be a nightmare. Maybe Skeele is right. Maybe we keep him starved of blood. But what if the bloodlust makes him crazy?

"No spoons," I say to Skeele and the other Hellion. It's not too hard to dig yourself out with a spoon; I've done it before. "No posters either." Only one of us can be channeling Andy Dufresne.

We walk back to the Hellion lair theorizing how to fix Sparrow and how the dead are getting into Heaven.

"We are going to help," I say, opening the door. "Gather whatever we need."

"We've never been freely allowed within the Seven Kingdoms of Heaven," Tukka says. "This will be something new."

"It's better for us to go than wait for the Archangels to come to us," I say. I will never wait for an invitation to justify myself again.

I always thought I'd battle everything with Sparrow at my side. That's how it's always been. Now I head off to a realm that despises me to finish a battle I didn't start, without him. It seems wrong. It seems off.

"Ready?" Chel asks.

"No." I tighten the leather that holds my blade. "Noah," I call.

He appears, looking solemn.

"I'm going to need you to stick by Skeele's side."

"Sure," he replies.

"And don't forget to feed the basilisk."

Noah makes a gagging sound.

"How are you going to travel between realms?" Skeele asks.

"Like I always have." I flick my fingers out. "With a poof. The Earthen plane is the only place that stops me."

I grip Chel and Tukka at their wrists. *Poof.* We go to the Seven Kingdoms of Heaven.

THE FAST ZOMBIE WAR

MEG

Chel and Tukka flinch at the brightness.

We all spin at the sound of a deep moan and motion behind us. Yup, the dead are walking here. They're walking fast. Two advance on us.

"Crap," I mutter, reaching for my blade.

Chel and Tukka move faster. They advance on the dead, chop off their heads, and kick the body parts away from each other.

I brought them to Babylon–neutral ground where the council meets. If we're lucky we can address all the Kings of the Seven Kingdoms.

"What happened to this place?" Chel asks.

Last time I was here the sidewalks glistened, the wicked were on display, and Babylon center was filled with angels going about their daily business.

Now there are streaks of blood staining the walkways. Bodies rotting. Little sparkle.

I try not to focus on the fact that they watched me kill and drain dry one of their own.

"Let's see if anyone's here." I head toward the large marble building nearby, remembering that the last time I approached this building there was a shackle around my neck and fresh wounds from a whipping across my back. I guess I haven't moved on. I'm really struggling with forgiveness.

Tukka grips the door, Chel stands ready for action. I take up the back, blade in hand. Tukka pulls the door open and we pause, listening for voices or footsteps. Chel nods for me to move inside. I take a few quick steps and take cover against a wall inside. The building is a mess, and it smells. Tukka makes sure the door is closed. The Hellions look very out of place here. I bet Remiel would roll over in his grave if he could see this: me roaming freely with Hellions in Babylon.

"Where are we going?" Chel asks.

"The courtroom." I point to a large door not far from us. "That's where they meet."

Tukka and Chel move forward, blades ready for action. I follow, alert and ready. Not only do we have to worry about the dead here, we have to worry about the angels.

"Ready?" Tukka grips the handle to the courtroom.

We nod.

Tukka pulls. The door creaks and he stops moving it as soon as the space is big enough for us to squeeze through without making more noise. I enter first.

The giant last supper-like table is still here. Seven chairs. No Archangels. Last time I was here I made a deal for Jack Cooper's soul and my freedom. I've spent far too much of my life fighting for my freedom. I shudder, remembering the Scarecrow's void of a face in this realm.

"Where are they?" Tukka asks.

"Not here." Losers. I guess they could be defending their king-doms. I shouldn't judge them too harshly. I was hoping to appeal my innocence once and assure them that the dead being here was not because of me. I guess that will have to wait.

"Well, boys, I guess we should move on." I tug Tukka and Chel closer. *Poof.* We go to Gabriel's Kingdom.

"Of all the bullshit," Gabriel shouts as something large falls and breaks glass.

We appear at the front door. Tukka shoves it open and we run in together. He's under attack. There have got to be twenty corpses walking around. Tukka and Chel start chopping. I turn, taking up the back and chop off the heads of the ones trying to sneak attack us.

"Meg?" Gabriel shouts. "Is that you?"

"Yes! We're here," I reply. "Head toward his voice," I tell Tukka.

My father's house is trashed. Glass is broken, paintings ripped, furniture busted to woodchips.

Gabriel is standing on the dining room table, taking on ten of the dead alone.

We work fast, making our way around the room. Blood sprays the walls. Heads fall with heavy *thwacks*. Jaws snap.

"Meg," Gabriel says as he jumps down from the table. "Thank God. You made it just in time to save dear old dad."

I smile. "Brought a few friends. We stopped in Babylon, but it was empty. I couldn't tell other Archangels that this is not my fault."

Gabriel shakes his head. "They're all fighting. The dead keep coming and they keep killing angels."

"Not turning them?" I ask.

"I haven't seen them change," Gabriel says. "Only die. I've lost many from my Kingdom. Nightingale has as well."

I look out the windows and listen for movement. "Where are the rest of your kingdom?" Last time I was here there were servants and staff keeping up the house.

"Hiding. I hid them. Came back here for weapons." Gabriel heads toward the kitchen. "I needed to get food for them." He opens the cabinets, grabs a bag off the counter that looks partially filled, and begins loading more inside. "Those walking corpses ambushed me."

"The fast ones seem to do that," I say.

Gabriel finishes filling the bag and turns to us. "I'm taking this back to them. They'll be fine in hiding here, but Nightingale needs help. Her kingdom is small. No Legion of their own." Gabriel glances at Chel and Tukka. "We are going to need more help than just the three of you."

"Okay," I'll get more help.

"I'm taking this back to my people." He secures the bag across his shoulder. "Get to Nightingale's Kingdom. The sooner the better."

"Okay," I nod. "See you soon."

Poof.

A Tisket, A tasket, A Basilisk in a Basket

We return to the Hellion's lair. It's empty. Chel and Tukka go behind the bar to get blood and power up. The door slams open and Skeele enters the room, securing the door closed behind him.

"Good, you're back," Skeele says.

"Not for long." I head for the wall of weapons to get another blade and guns. "We have to go back."

"I'm not sure if now is a good time," Skeele says. It's the tone of his voice that causes me to pause and focus on the noises in the hallway behind the closed door.

"Skeele?" I ask.

"They're here," he says.

Shit.

"How is this happening?" I ask, shoving a handgun into my belt.

"They're coming through the portals. They've never been able to cross before," Skeele says.

"How do we stop them?" I ask. "Close up the portals? What?"

"We could," Skeele says, running toward the weapons and grabbing ammo and securing small blades on his belt. "If we close the portals, no one can travel between realms but those with your ability to *poof*. Then we'd still have to deal with the ones that are here."

"Blast the portals. Kill the dead that don't belong," I say. My stomach growls. "Noah," I call.

He appears.

"I need something to eat. Something sweet. Like Cinnabons or donuts or something."

"I was just feeding the basilisk." Noah wipes his hands on his pants. "One of those dead things came running in the office and I spilled their food. Hold your nose if you enter."

"Did you kill it?" I ask.

Noah shakes his head. "Didn't have to. Momma ate it."

"Wait, the basilisk eat the walking dead?" I'm suddenly no longer hungry.

"Just the fast ones, it seems," Noah says.

An idea is forming. It seems nuts but being nuts has gotten us this far.

"Leave one portal open," I tell Skeele. "The closest one to us."

"Meg?" he asks.

"We are taking them on a field trip." This is going to suck.

Poof. I check on Sparrow. He's still locked up. Still looking dead. The Hellion assigned to him appears eager to be elsewhere. I check on Jed and Shay. They've got the bedroom door secured and coated the room in spells.

"Watch where you're walking," Jed scolds as my boot scuffs the black hieroglyphs on the floor. He bends to fix the marking. "I prefer not to die in the middle of this."

"Sorry. I was just checking in," I say.

"You're all going?" Shay asks.

"We should be back soon." *Poof.* I go to my grandfather's

office. The basket we moved the babies in is on the floor next to the tank. Klaus is there and he doesn't look thrilled.

I pick up the basket. "Remember what we did last time?" I ask. "We are going to do it again."

A slithering sound echoes from the ceiling. We're making momma anxious.

I dip the basket in the tank of water and move the baby basilisk. Hissing warns us but doesn't stop me.

"You ready to run?" I ask Klaus.

He makes a grim face.

"Noah," I call. "You're coming with us!"

Klaus grips the other side of the basket and we take off running for the front door. The momma basilisk follows. Part of me feels shitty baiting her with her babies. It's kinda cruel to do to a mother.

We run out of the office, down the hallway, down the stairs, and toward the front door that's carved out of the caves. Skeele is waiting with a running Jeep.

Noah flashes to the passenger seat. "I call shotgun."

Klaus helps me secure the basket in the cargo area and we scramble into the backseat. "Go, go, go!" we both shout at Skeele.

Skeele burns rubber, speeding away, turning right onto the nearest crumbling road.

"How far?" I ask.

"I can make it in ten minutes," Skeele says, determined. The Jeep lurches as he presses harder on the gas pedal.

The mother basilisk rounds the corner and flies toward us. She's a little faster this time, not letting us get too far ahead.

***

Skeele turns into an old graveyard. There's an arch in the distance, similar to the portals we've used elsewhere. He parks the Jeep with a skid and a jerk. We scramble out. Skeele and Klaus grab the basket o' babies. Tukka and Chel are waiting for us.

The mother basilisk moves closer.

"Wait until the last minute," Klaus suggests. "We don't want her to turn away."

For a split second I remember I've been banished from Heaven. I wonder what will happen when I show up there again. I don't have much time to think about it. The basilisk's sharp teeth are close enough to bite off our faces. We run through.

<hr>

The portal drops us in a field. There's a castle in the distance, but not my father's or Nightingale's. Wonderful. There's nothing worse than not knowing whose backyard you've fallen into. Knowing these Archangels, I don't trust that they'll let us help them.

An arrow whizzes by and lands in Chel's thigh. "What the hell?" he shouts.

"Run," I suggest.

We head for a line of trees, the basket sloshing and basilisk babies squealing.

A dead man exits the tree line in front of us. He's walking quick, nearly running.

Something drips out of the sky. We look up to see the momma basilisk fly over us, swoop in, and grab the walking corpse in her mouth. She swallows it down.

"I have an idea," I tell the Hellions. "Get to Nightingale's Kingdom. Noah will show you where it is. I'll be right back." I wretch the basket of babies out of their hands and, *poof*, I go back to Hell.

I empty the baby basilisk into the tank and set the basket on the floor for later.

Poof. I return to where I left the Hellions. I was only gone a few minutes but they're not here. I hear crashing from the forest. It's either the dead or the Hellions, or the momma Basilisk tearing this place apart.

Nightingale's Kingdom isn't far. I poof from place to place, looking for the Hellions and the basilisk. Finally, I *poof* to Nightingale's castle.

The front door is broken. Thick wood is cracked and hinges bent. Nightingale's castle is under attack. I get a glimpse of the basilisk's tail through the front windows. I grip my blade and run up the steps to the front door. It's open. There's screaming, moaning, and crashing inside.

"Nightingale?" I shout as I enter the castle.

I hear a baby cry. Skeele's deep voice shouts something unintelligible. I follow the noise. There's blood everywhere. More noise coming from upstairs. I head that way, taking the stairs two at a time.

"Jack?" I shout, hoping someone can give me some guidance.

Sounds of battle come from each end of the hallway once I reach the top of the stairs. I go toward Nightingale's room.

Which way do I go? I'm not sure if I should turn left, but I do. This looks as bad as the damage on the Earthen plane. At least there was a little warning and time to prepare on that plane. People have been prepping for apocalypse conditions for decades there. Not the Seven Kingdoms of Heaven. No, Heaven has been basking in their righteousness and glory. The dead coming was like a hotel bathtub kidney removal after a night of heavy drinking with a pretty girl met on the internet. Unexpected.

Walls are busted in, expensive furniture broken, thick carpets torn to shreds.

I run to the room with the most noise.

Things happen fast after I step into the room. Skeele throws a dagger at the back of a dead man's head. The dead man trips. The dagger hits the wall. The dead man falls into Nightingale. Jack shouts. Nightingale tosses baby Thrush like a basketball toward Jack. He moves to catch the baby but notices Night about to be bit. Jack reaches for both. *Poof.* I catch Thrush. Jack goes for Night. The ceiling caves in. Four of the dead fall on Jack. Two bite his neck. Then one bites Nightingale on her cheek. The basilisk slides in the hole of the ceiling, eating as she goes. Noah screams, a noise like I've never heard. He roars like a pained lion, white light illuminates around him. My heart sinks.

Poof. I take Thrush to Hell.

Tiny Visitor

I appear in Jed and Shay's room with a crying baby.

"What the heck?" Shay asks as she stands.

I run across the room and thrust the baby into Jed's arms. "No time to talk. Protect this kid with everything you've got."

Poof. I go back to Nightingale's.

Skeele is checking pulses. Noah is bent over Nightingale's pale, crumpled form, gripping her tightly. They don't have to tell me; they're both gone. There was a time in my life that I didn't give a shit about anyone or anything. My heart aches like never before.

"Where did the basilisk go?" I ask.

"Out the window," Tukka waves. "To eat more."

I nod, feeling sick. I want to puke and cry at the same time. I can do neither.

Poof. I go to my father.

Gabriel is picking up furniture and making a pile of the broken stuff in the grass outside his door. He takes one look at me and stops what he's doing. "What happened?"

I tell him. The portals tend to just drop you somewhere if you don't give it directions, not always the same place. Fields, churches, bathrooms. You never know. I'm sure that hasn't helped here either. Kinda hard to prepare when a handful of zombies fall out of the sky. At least, that's what I think happened.

"Mother of pearl." He rubs his face and sits on the stairs of the wraparound porch.

I walk toward him and he pulls me down to sit next to him, one arm wrapped tight around my shoulders.

"What happens to them?" I ask.

"When the soul is extinguished, you simply cease to exist," he replies, solemn.

I wipe my eyes. "They won't come back?"

Gabriel shakes his head. "Not even Teari could have healed those wounds. I'm sure she's with them, up in the stars somewhere. Never thought I'd see a mess like this in my time."

I shake my head. "I didn't do this. Do the other Archangels know?"

He shakes his head. I should've known when Chel got arrowed in the leg.

"I'll leave the basilisk until it cleans everything up." I stand. "I have to go back to Hell now. The fast dead are growing in numbers there."

"We'll come help, just... give us a moment to collect the Legion or what's left of them," he offers. "But, you know what this means now?" he asks.

"What?"

"With Nightingale and Jack gone, Sparrow's now the king, until Thrush becomes of age."

Something sinks deep in my gut like a stone in mud.

"Their Kingdom cannot sit empty for long," he warns, squeezing my shoulder one last time before releasing me. "Go back to your realm. We'll be there soon."

The Liar

S hit got real fucked up. I thought it was before, but this is next level.

The Hellions secure the main doors and clear the castle. We are safe in here, for now. We have patrols, security, and spells—thanks to Jed. The lesser demons are scouting Hell for more, but the portals are demolished. Only one remains.

I sit at the end of the Hellions bar, staring at a glass of blood. I swallow a gulp and do better at controlling the reaction of lust. I don't have to leave the room this time, but I cross my legs tight and think of the basilisk babies roiling in their basket. That's enough to change the mood trying to bloom in my lower abdomen.

"How do you think it happened?" Skeele asks.

"On the Earthen plane, me and Teari had found Sparrow. They were bit. Blood was dripping down the stone wall we were perched on. And the dead licked it like a lollipop." I push the glass away, disgusted with myself. "They drank Sparrow's blood. They drank Teari's blood. And it turned those dead souls into something we've never seen before."

Skeele nods as he takes it all in. "So Sparrow's blood is next level, huh?" He smirks. "No wonder you rarely come for the cheap stuff."

I make a face. He doesn't really have a clue what Sparrow's blood does to me. Better than a moon's over my hammy with bacon from Denny's. Better than the finest liquor served ocean-side at a little bar in Key West. Better than Thanksgiving dinner at a real home where the grandma makes everything from scratch. These past few months, I've pined over him. I've remembered how wonderful it would feel to have him in my bed again. To share the bloodlust. To finally be together again. Now I'm not sure if we'll ever return to that. The tables have turned and suddenly I fully understand the phrase *you can't go back home.*

I was once a child and Sparrow was supposed to watch over me. He messed up and fled. And here we are now. Sparrow is mine and I am his. And he will be my walking dead man until I can figure out how to fix him.

Skeele walks to the fridge and gets more blood. He pours glasses for the others. There are new recruits in the Hellion barracks. We had to strengthen the numbers. The new ones make me uneasy. They're scarred and horned and colored various shades of reds and browns. They're unpredictable and wild like Hellions of old. They need more training, but there isn't time.

"Keep your chin up," Skeele reminds me.

I tip my head and try to not get lost in the memories of the old Meg. It's so easy to get sucked down into that spiral and put up the walls around me.

"I'm going to need a rum and coke," I say.

"Liquid courage?" Skeele doesn't change his expression. He knows the new ones are watching. He makes the drink and slides it across the bar to me.

I down the rum and coke, then stand. I grip my blade as I move to the center of the room.

"Listen up!" I start. "There's a swarm outside the north entry. We're going to clear it. Bring only blades. No guns. They're fast. They don't belong here. These are not our dead." I reach for the door. "Remember, nothing gets to the third floor."

The Hellions follow me, Skeele at my side as my first in command. It should be Sparrow.

Chel and a new recruit shove open the heavy wooden door. We have about twenty feet to the barricade fence the Hellions built. Ten feet tall and topped with barbed wire and cement barricades, it looks like something from the Cold War. Some of the Hellions take to the sky, their bat-like wings blocking out the dull sun as they slay the dead. I circle a path near the door, jabbing my blade through the fence into skulls as needed. I won't say that I don't trust them to keep the inside of the castle secure. They don't know what the third floor holds. They don't know that I have a baby from the Seven Kingdoms of Heaven in hiding. I was once hidden on a different realm. I didn't think I would ever do it to another child. Seems I am no better than my history.

I check on baby Thrush, Jed, and Shay. I knock three times on the door and give Jed time to clear the runes off the doorway so I can enter. Thrush has Nightingale's dark hair and Noah's blue eyes. He's sleeping in an old crib Noah found at an empty house in Buffalo. Noah sits near the window, his handsome face drawn. I don't know if he'll ever get over losing Nightingale. At least before he could see her in the Astral. Now none of us will again.

"Do you need anything for him?" I whisper, afraid to wake Thrush.

"Diapers," Shay whispers back. "Unexpired formula would be good. Or if you have goat milk."

"Hell isn't known for goats," I reply.

"Have the fast ones stopped?" Jed asks.

I shake my head. "Not yet." Being in this room makes me uneasy. "I've got to go." I motion to the marks on the floor. "Fix this."

"I always do," Jed says.

I leave, rubbing my face as I take the short walk down the hall to my room. I push open the door, close it, lean against the carved wood, and slide to the floor. What a mess.

Gabriel arrives in a flash of light.

I hear Skeele's footsteps outside my door. He's the only one allowed up here now.

"Hey, Meg," my father says. "I've got the Legion ready." He looks tired. We are all tired.

I stand. "That's good. The realm of Hell thanks you."

"It's the least we could do after you lent us that snake thing." He motions to the sky and rotates his finger.

"It's a basilisk," I say.

Gabriel shivers. "It's disgusting."

"Does the job though. Is it done up there?" I ask. "I'll have to get the Hellions together to go back and get it."

Gabriel paces near the window. "It should be done soon. There haven't been reports of the fast dead in a few days."

"Did you destroy your portals?" I ask. "A single point of entry has helped."

Gabriel nods.

A yellow flicker lands on the railing of the balcony. The songbirds are wondering what happened to their daily feedings. I walk to the bag of seed, scoop out a handful and scatter it on the balcony railing. I pause for a moment, watching smoke rise from the portal in the distance. The Hellions are burning the bodies. We used to welcome the souls. We used to count our strength on their numbers. Now we just want them to stop.

Gabriel clears his throat.

I sigh, knowing some bullshit is coming. "What?" I ask.

"The other kingdoms will not be sending help." Gabriel runs his fingers through his long white beard.

"No? After all I've done for them?" I say.

"They want to blame someone. They aren't fully convinced it wasn't you."

"I told you what happened. This was an accident. Who knew? And I'd like to go back in time and bring up the fact that the Seven Kingdoms of Heaven hired the Scarecrow to find me on the Earthen plane. If they hadn't started meddling in my life, this would have never happened."

Gabriel raises his brows and smirks. "That's my girl. Don't let this burn out your fire."

"Sure," I reply. I just wanted to take a shower and get some clean clothes on. I'm not sure why I always do that. I guess maybe it's because I went so long without hot showers and clean clothes. "I guess if the Kingdoms of Michael, Raphael, Raguel, Uriel, and Phanuel don't want to help me, I'll just go get the basilisk and let them clean up their kingdoms alone," I say.

"If you must." He watches songbirds collect on the railing and whistles a short trill.

I pause. Waiting. That was something Nightingale and Sparrow would do. Not my father. My heart is still heavy with sorrow for losing Nightingale. Funny how a little whistle could mean so much.

"Hm," Gabriel finally says. "I was hoping something would whistle back."

"They haven't gotten much interaction here lately," I remind him. "The birds are skittish."

Gabriel nods. "I'm going to get the Legion. Make sure your Hellions don't try to kill us as soon as we arrive."

"I'll do my best," I say.

"Oh, and one thing..."

"Yeah?" I ask.

"They're looking for Nightingale's baby. Do you know where he went?"

I keep my face placid. "No clue." I lie.

Gabriel nods slowly. "We've lost many these few weeks." He pauses, waiting for me to speak. I say nothing. "I'll be back soon," he finally says.

Poof. He's gone.

I sit at the balcony, stare off into the Hellsky, and think.

There's a knock on my door.

"What?" I shout.

The door cracks open and I recognize Skeele's shadow. "Are you alone now?"

"Yes." I take off my jacket and toss it across the room on the chair before working on unlacing my boots.

He enters the room.

"What?" I ask again, annoyed.

"You shouldn't just let him come and go as he pleases." Skeele's brow is furrowed in concern.

"He's my father. He's of no worry to us." I get my left boot off and toss it aside before starting on the next.

"He is a king from the Seven Kingdoms of Heaven." Skeele steps closer. "You shouldn't be alone with him."

"Just stop." I shake my head in annoyance. "I don't need a babysitter. I can handle my father."

"But can you? Have you seen him at his worst? Have you seen the power of an Archangel who has been around for eons?"

I toss my right boot and stand. I'm taller than most but Skeele still towers over me. "I'm not afraid of him." I start unbuttoning my overshirt.

"You shouldn't be alone," Skeele lowers his voice.

I pause.

"I already have a boyfriend. I don't need another," I say.

Guilt floods me. Skeele has helped even when I hated him and let him know it. He's never left my side. He's always been there. He offered to feed me and cared for me while I healed from falling out of the sky. He's probably seen too much of me. I stop unbuttoning the shirt and drop my hands.

"You shouldn't be alone when he can drop by, unannounced, at any time." Skeele steps closer and grips the blade at his hip. "Someone should always be with you."

"I've been alone for plenty of my life."

"You need to be fed. You need—" Skeele pauses abruptly.

"What do you think I need?" I ask.

Oh, this is not good. I know Sparrow was feeding off random women and god knows what else he was doing. I'm not a fan of what he did to survive. But, I should be able to do what I want; the draw is there. I'd like to have a warm body in my bed at night. Someone to worship me in the midnight hours. I've had plenty of boyfriends before. Some who have hung around longer than others. Look at Noah. Although, he can't help it.

Skeele's eyes are fire as they take me in from head to toe. "There has never been a female ruler here. There has never been a female who will fight on the battlefield with us. Hellions are better than they used to be, but still..."

I let out a laugh but stop abruptly as he tips his head to the side. It's a very Sparrow-like move and makes me wonder if maybe Sparrow was never bird-like in his mannerisms. Maybe he was always Hellion-like in his movements.

"I still haven't forgiven you for dropping me out of the sky." I brush a hand over my shoulder. Memories and anger bubble in my chest. "No wings. Still. If you'd like to bring it down a few notches, remember that. There's not much great about me. So stop trying to pressure me into believing the Hellions give a fuck about what I am. I know what they are. I know what you are." I jab a finger in his direction. "I know what I came from. I know what I am. I am a liar, and a sinner, and a fuck up. Look at this mess I've created and you want me to hold my chin up like some pathological asshole. I am not like my grandfather." My fingertips tingle with anger. He's lucky I don't have my blade near or I just might stab him.

"They'd come out if you'd let them." His wings unfold a tiny bit to tease me.

"Get lost, jackass," I dismiss him then turn and walk toward the bathroom.

Heavy footsteps come after me. A giant hand wraps around my upper arm and tugs me to face him. Skeele is right there. His face inches from mine.

Something throbs in my core. I know what it is. Desire. I had it for Sparrow. Still have it for him. After that night of dancing before he got turned into zombie-boy, there was never any relief. And here I've been, walking around for weeks ready to pop.

Skeele isn't that bad. I've seen worse. The horns don't scare me anymore. And to tell the truth, when I woke to find him reading a newspaper at the end of the bed all those months ago, it was an image I couldn't get out of my head. Skeele's not like the others. He's not like the old pack of Hellions that did terrible things to me before I knew what I was. I shouldn't have said those words a moment ago.

He reaches forward with his free hand and tugs at the buttons to my shirt. They pop off and scatter across the floor, revealing the tank top underneath.

"I watched you heal from a sack of broken bones to this," Skeele says, his voice low, eyes half-lidded. "I sat at your bedside for months. Watching your every breath." He drops to one knee. "Please, Meg, let me be of use to you."

Now, I've done plenty bad in my life. I cheated and took what wasn't mine. I didn't start changing until Sparrow came into my life and I never tried to be better. He's been gone all this time. He fed off other women. We never promised anything to each other. And now I don't know if I'll ever have Sparrow again.

"Please, Meg," Skeele whispers again.

What would Andy Dufresne do? What would Sparrow do? What would Bon Jovi do? I close my eyes. What would Meg do? Why do I always rely on the morals of men? Men do what they want. They take what they want. Why can't I? There was that one Bon Jovi song about a cheating dude. Sparrow sang it to me before...

Skeele holds out his wrist.

I see the throb of his veins and arteries. I suck in a breath. I've never had Hellion before. Skeele rises to his feet and holds his wrist closer to my mouth.

"You need your strength for what we are about to embark on," he urges. "Use me."

Damn. What do you do when a monster begs you to use them like a piece of raw meat?

I grab his arm and sink my teeth into his wrist.

BURNT

The shower is boiling hot as I wet my face and scrub the blood off. Red stains the water as it slides down the drain. My gut is full. My brain buzzing. I feel like I did a line of cocaine. I scrub my body, my hand lingering in the vee between my legs. Christ. That could have gone in a very different direction. It's hard to control the lust. I'm getting better at it. At least, I think I am.

I wash my hair and turn off the shower. Wrapping myself in towels, I dry myself in record time. No lingering. We've got shit to do. I leave my short hair damp to air dry and head to the closet. Knowing we'll be fighting, I grab leather pants, knee high boots, a thin undershirt, and leather jacket. The fit is good for movement and the extra leather should protect my skin if one of the dead tries to bite me. I glance at my bag. I grab it and throw a change of clothes in there. Since Noah is busy with other things, I'll have to get my own snacks. Heck, I'm lazy. Maybe I'll just skip the snacks. I feel like I could last a few days after fresh blood.

"Child?" Clea arrives near the window.

"Yea?" I ask, leaving the closet.

"Your father is coming?" she asks.

"He is," I nod. "He's going to help us."

"The Legion has never helped Hell in all of history. This will be new." Her ruby red lips press together in concern. "You look strong. Even without Sparrow by your side. You can help set this right."

"I sent the basilisk to Heaven to help them," I remind her.

Clea nods.

"Why are you really here?" I ask.

"Sparrow doesn't look good. I think he's getting worse." She fidgets with her gown. Pale fingers tracing the white embroidery.

"I know." My shoulders drop. "We must clear the realm before I can figure out how to fix him. Unless you have any ideas," I say.

She folds her hands. "I've none. Only concern for him and that room I cannot enter." She points to the wall.

Jed's spells are good. Noah is sworn to secrecy, he wouldn't do anything to hurt his own child. And since Thrush is all that he has left of Nightingale, Noah is on his best behavior.

I secure my bag across my shoulder. "Are you coming to fight with us?" I ask. "We could use the extra numbers. Gabriel doesn't have many Legion left and I'm going to feel really bad if he loses more down here."

Clea watches out the window. "I'll go. Since I've got nothing else to do." She disappears in a puff of smoke.

I secure my blade with the holster on my thigh and settle the bag over my shoulder. I circle the room, taking it in. It's hard to escape the feeling that I might never see this room again. I'm headed to war, well, back into war. A war with the fast-dead.

I leave the bedroom and make my way down the long hall and the winding stone stairwell. The familiar smell of woodsmoke and pine is thick in the air now that the castle is locked up and secured.

I roll my shoulders and try to set my mind straight. I said some shit to Skeele and then used him like a Slurpee machine. I reminded him that I hate Hellions. Old wounds are hard to bury. Now I have to step into war with them. I cinch the strap holding my blade a little tighter. These new Hellions are wild and I doubt Skeele, Chel, Tukka, or Klaus could stop them from turning on us. I've been on the receiving end of Hellions doing their worst. I can't let it happen again.

War And Regret

There is a vibrating energy to the Hellions' lair. They're fed, briefed, and ready to fight.

"Only kill the fast ones. The slow ones belong here. They are not the same. There will be Legion present from Gabriel's kingdom. Don't kill them. Don't eat them. They are here to help." I glance at Skeele. He doesn't look like he lost any blood, like I nearly drained him dry upstairs a few hours ago.

"We don't need their help," one of the new recruits mutters from the back.

"Hey," Chel says from the shadows, his voice low and threatening. "You'll take their help and thank them."

"We clear the realm. Then they go back," I say. "Klaus and Chel will stay to protect the castle. You all are coming with Skeele and Tukka." I pause for dramatic effect. "And me."

You could hear a pin drop.

We head for the door, Skeele walking by my side. He pushes open the giant, carved door at the base of the burning caves. The Hellions take to the air to get over the barricade.

Chel and Klaus wait at the mouth of the cave.

"Nothing gets to the third floor," I remind them.

Klaus tips his head. "What's so special about the third floor all of a sudden?"

"None of your business." I *poof* to the other side of the fence. It's been a long time since I've felt this powerful. Maybe Skeele was right. Maybe all I needed was a little fresh blood from a dark creature.

There are about ten bodies that the Hellions have already taken care of. They pull the corpses to a pile and set them on fire.

Hearing footsteps, I turn quickly to find Skeele walking toward me. It's intimidating; tall, muscled, leaning forward like a cat ready to pounce as he walks. He's decked out in Hellion gear, leathers and straps securing various weapons. His wings twitch in anticipation of flying.

The others take to the sky and survey from above.

"Why aren't you flying?" I ask Skeele.

"I could ask you the same," he replies with a dark grin.

"Don't," I warn.

"Would you like me to carry you," he points to Hellsky, "up there?"

"Nope." I grip my blade, ready to use it on any fast ones that come out of the surrounding forests. Or Skeele. "Is Gabriel here with the Legion?"

"Yes." He points in the direction of the last portal. "They are not far. We should be meeting them soon."

We walk in silence for miles.

"We could have driven," Skeele finally says.

"Nah, then we'd miss them." I point at myself. "Bait."

On cue a zombie runs out of the tree line. Before I can do anything, one of the Hellions drops from the sky and slices it down the middle. Two more drop down to grab the parts, toss them in a pile, and light them on fire.

Skeele makes a hand signal to the ones above and we keep walking. "Portal's up here," he says.

"I know," I say. "I remember. Been down here long enough."

"I was just–"

A blast rocks the ground and smoke rises from the direction where Skeele had just pointed.

"Gabriel!" I take off running as fast as I can.

This can't be good. A million things run through my mind. I've already lost Nightingale and Jack. And there's a strong chance I might lose Sparrow and Teari. I can't lose Gabriel too. They can't leave me to navigate this alone.

With Skeele's blood pumping through my veins, I run faster.

BIRD IN A CAGE

The portal is gone. The only thing left is a giant dirt hole in the ground. Dark dirt like a giant bowl pressed in the soil, littered with a few rocks from what was the portal.

"Gabriel!" I shout.

A dozen or so of the fast dead come running out of the surrounding forest. The Hellions get to work. Heads fall, limbs drop. The Hellions split most down the middle so they can't reanimate while they burn.

"Did he come through?" I ask one of the new Hellions. "Did Gabriel or any of the Legion come through?"

"There was no one," the Hellion says. "We were in the air when we saw the explosion."

Poof. I go to my father's kingdom.

Something's not right. Dad's acting sketchy. I knock on the giant embossed door only to find it's open. The house is put back together. In such a short time? It smells like fresh paint and lacquer and baked bread. "Gabriel?" I call. No one answers. This house is empty. I walk through the middle hall and check all the rooms, through the kitchen and out the back door, down through the vast yard to the Legion barracks. The Legion training grounds. It's all empty.

Poof. I go to Sparrow's old house in the woods. It's empty too, but I'd expect it to be.

Poof. I go to Nightingale's house. It's burned to the ground. The giant skeleton of the basilisk is set within the ashes, bones charred to ochre. The ash smells familiar. But I am used to the smells of Hell now.

Poof. I go to Babylon.

"No!" a familiar voice shouts. "Get out of here, Meg!"

In the distance, I see Gabriel in a cage, much like I was once, a gleaming tall cage in the bright sunlight. There's no missing it. Sweat beads his brow and his hair glistens wet. His robes are gone.

"Get out of here!" he shouts, his eyes wide.

He doesn't have to tell me three times.

Poof. I go back to Hell.

Everything Falls
Apart

"Where did you go?" Skeele asks.

"To find Gabriel." I try to dry my sweaty palms on my pants but they slide across the leather. "He's imprisoned. He won't be helping us."

I scan the perimeter of the field. The slow dead halt at my presence and waver behind the shadows. Others come through fast, jaws snapping. Angry, I ready my blade and go to work, helping the other Hellions. Dozens more than I saw in Nightingale's kingdom. When they finally stop, I help the Hellions drag the body parts to a burn pile. I am covered in gore and ichor. Rotting blood coats my pants from the splatter. The smell of the burning bodies fills the air. I hold back a gag.

Poof. I go back to my room. The castle is quiet. Jed's spells keep the sounds of baby Thrush inside the room next door. What a mess. I strip off my clothes and rinse myself off in the shower. I need to think. I need to figure out what to do. I wrap myself in a towel then head to the closet to find more clothes. I dress in record time.

Poof. I go back to the field. Tukka and Skeele are circling the field in the sky. Their giant bat-like wings block out the fading sunlight. I approach the nearest Hellion.

"Hey," I call to one with curled horns like a mountain ram. "Have any more of the fast ones come this way?"

"No," the Hellion replies.

"And all of the other portals were destroyed?" I ask.

"As far as we know. The Deacons were pissed that they no longer had the ability to move between realms and consult the Seven Kingdoms of Heaven," the Hellion says.

Goddamned Deacons. Those bastards have been nothing but a thorn in my side.

Skeele lands near me and walks closer.

"I'm going to check the other portals. And make sure the Deacons haven't rebuilt one," I head for the road.

Skeele nods. "We'll finish up here."

I walk down the center of route 54, headed for Interstate 81. The moon is my only light. My stomach growls and for a moment I wish Noah was still at my beck and call to feed me like a nice handsome butler. I don't see us returning to those days any time soon. I shouldn't have used my power to travel so much. It makes me hungry and there is no Hellion lair fridge with blood here. I'll have to suffer. It's fine. I can do it.

The sound of a car on the road interrupts the silence around me. I move to the shoulder and keep walking. It could be a lost soul who found a car, searching for answers like I once did. It seems like forever ago I was searching this plane with Sparrow. Forever ago I thought I knew everything but knew nothing at all. I didn't know who I was, I didn't know what I was. But Sparrow searching for that Snowy Owl was the distraction I needed. I can't remember the last time I picked up a feather. It's probably a good thing. Most brought visions of something terrible. I don't think I'll ever trust a feather again.

The car slows. "Want a ride?"

I turn to see Skeele in the Jeep. He stops, reaches across the passenger seat, and opens the door. "Get in."

Tired and hungry, he doesn't have to ask twice.

"You're going to check them all?" Skeele asks as I close the door.

"Yup." I glance at him. "You didn't want to fly or walk?"

"I knew you wouldn't fly. And I'm not about to walk the entire way." He shifts the Jeep into drive and accelerates.

It's a few hours to check the portal in Saratoga. It's dismantled. Not as badly as the one that was bombed near the burning caves, but close. The rocks from the archway are strewn about and broken down to dust in some places.

"The last one is across the Vermont border," Skeele reminds me.

My stomach growls. "What I wouldn't give for a platter of gas station nachos and a blue Slurpee."

"There's a place to stay up here," Skeele motions ahead of us to the mountain across the valley.

"What kind of place?"

"Where Hellions can stay when they're out on patrol. It's not much, but we can rest and there's food."

"Okay," I agree.

It's not long before he pulls into the driveway of an old cabin. It looks like it was once a bed a breakfast tucked into the mountainside. Cobwebs string from porch railings and a pale bulb flickers near the door.

We get out of the Jeep and Skeele walks up to the front door and opens it.

"No locks?" I ask.

He laughs. "Hellions don't need locks."

That thinking is what got my door broken down. I'll have to remember it.

It's spacious. Dusty. Reminds me of the Hellion lair back at the burning caves. I kick the door closed and head for the giant bed tucked into the corner. I take off my bag and drop it on the night-stand before flopping onto the bed and falling asleep.

I dream of Sparrow. It's filthy. We're naked and sweating and feeding off each other. His blood is warm in my mouth. Delicious. It coats my throat and fills my stomach. It fills one need. There's another that comes with the bloodlust. A throb deep in my lower abdomen takes over. I throw a leg over Sparrow and take the lead. I've waited so long to have him like this. To be filled with him. It feels so good and I'm impatient. His hands are on my body, my hips, gripping and pinching my skin in all the right places. I rotate my hips and–

"Wake up," Sparrow says. "Wake up. Wake up. Wake up."

My eyes flash open.

It's not Sparrow.

It's Skeele. His eyes are half-lidded and his hands are around my waist.

"The hunger will never go away. If you don't do something about it, you're going to do something you regret."

Seems Skeele was right. Fuck.

The Vermont portal is a two-hour drive. We encounter five of the fast dead on our way there. Skeele pulls over and tells me he'll take care of them. There is no chivalry in Hell. I get out and take one of them out.

"I said I'd get it," Skeele says as we drag them to a pile on the side of the road and light their carcasses on fire.

"I am not some maiden who waits in a car while you pump gas," I say. "This is my realm."

"It is your realm. And a Hellion protects their leader. It is my duty." He sounds pissed as he marches back to the Jeep and gets behind the wheel.

More silence.

I never knew the Hellions to be so moody. I've only known them to act on impulse and fuck shit up. Hm. Kinda sounds like me... Skeele hasn't been like that though. Neither have the others. I'm going to have to change my method of thinking. I wonder if there's therapists in Hell.

Skeele turns onto a dirt road after passing a sign for Green Mountain National Forest.

He stops the Jeep and we get out to inspect the ruins in the clearing.

This portal is demolished as well.

Annoyed at the mood and the lack of a portal for the fast-dead to come through, I decide to go elsewhere, alone.

Poof. I go back to the burning caves and leave Skeele to find his own way back.

I run down the winding stone stairs to the dungeon below. I turn right. Go straight, don't look at the creatures caged there. I run to Sparrow's door at the end. I peer at him through the barred window.

"Has he eaten?" I ask the Hellion stationed at his door.

"Nothing," is the reply.

"No blood?" I ask.

"No," the Hellion says.

Sparrow's skin is gray, his green eyes dull and milky. His dark hair is matted and oily. He turns at the sound of my voice. His jaw bites. He scuffs toward the door.

"Sparrow?" I ask. "How do I fix this?"

"He won't answer you," the Hellion says. "Can't speak a word, just grunts and moans and snaps."

I ignore the Hellion. "Tell me how to fix this," I say through the bars. Sparrow's teeth snap loudly and echo against the stone walls of his cell.

Out of all the movies I've watched, none can help me with this mess. Shawshank never turned into this clusterfuck. Andy Dufresne would roll over in his grave.

Sparrow always said we would be invincible together, but not like this. We cannot be invincible as he rots in a cell. I must figure out how to release him from this curse. The laws of the ethereal realms kept tearing us apart. Or maybe I keep tearing us apart. Maybe we were never meant to stay together, like Gabriel and Clea. Me and Sparrow could be nothing but a tragedy. Could I forgive him? Even if I fix him, could he forgive me? I did lose his book, after all. *Birds of Paradise* is nothing but a needle in a haystack here. I've known some people who would never speak to you again if you lost their book.

Skeele's blood has given me power. *Poof* – I ignore the warnings of weeks ago and blast through to the Earthen realm.

Things We Left Behind

The hospital is still open, the barricades and military thinned to a single crew. The parking lot has a few more cars in it than last time. I walk to the emergency room doors and go inside.

"There is only one inpatient," the lady at the desk says and gives me directions to the room.

The elevator works. I take it to the second floor and pass empty rooms until I get to the big corner one.

I knock on the door before pushing it open.

Teari is sitting in a chair eating hospital food.

"You left me in Scranton, Pennsylvania," Teari scowls. "Of all places."

"What's wrong with Scranton?" I ask, looking out the window.

"It's cold." Teari throws her blankets off her legs and walks toward a cupboard on the wall. Using the nubs of her arms, she opens the cupboard with a rope that's tied around the handle and pulls out her clothes. "Help me get out of this disgusting gown."

I pat my pack. "I brought you clean clothes."

"I hope they're not hand me downs from you. You're much shorter than I am. I like my pants to cover my ankles."

"Beggars can't be choosers." I unzip my bag and pull out the clothes. "I actually stopped at Wal-Mart before coming here. They didn't have a women's big and tall section, but the men's had some good choices."

"Ugh," Teari scoffs.

I'm sure she's not thrilled to slum it in cheap clothes. She's always been dressed to the nines or in expensive combat gear. T-shirts and sweats don't quite compare.

Teari tries to take the bag from my hand. Since she's got no fingers, I drop the bag on the bed and sort through it, laying out all the items I bought for her. She motions to a few pieces. "I'm going to need some help," she says holding up her arms.

I untie the hospital gown and leave it loose.

"I thought you'd love these grannie panties," I joke as I hold out the underwear for her to step into. "And these big white socks are straight out of 1986. It's all they had. I promise." I kneel and hold the socks open for her to put her feet into. She picked out a pair of loose sweatpants. I hold them open for her to step into.

"Don't tie them," Teari warns. "I can't do the ties."

I nod and gather the T-shirt, putting it over her head before pulling the hospital gown away. The nurses in Gouverneur taught me how to get dressed like that. After, I help her into a zip-up hoodie.

"You want me to roll the sleeves?" I ask. The sleeve fabric just sways loose, unfilled because of her missing hands.

She shakes her head. "I'm just going to the bathroom before we go," Teari says.

I sit in a chair by the window and wait for her. I can't imagine going to the bathroom without hands. I wonder if she's drip-drying. My questions are answered when I hear her sniff and hiccup, doing her best to cry softly.

I shift in my chair, uncomfortable with the crying Angel.

Comforting someone is not my strong suite. Heck, I don't think I've ever comforted a person in my life. At least nothing more than a few pats on the back from an arm's length away.

Teari finally leaves the bathroom. I avoid looking at her face. I don't want her to feel like she has to explain the puffy eyes or redness.

"Get me the heck out of here," Teari says.

I hold up a finger. "Shoes. We almost forgot shoes."

"The hospital slippers are tempting," Teari says. "I can't really tie any laces."

"But I've got these." I open another bag and hold up a pair of slides. "Easy." I drop them on the floor in front of her.

I show her the way out and find a car in the parking lot with the keys still in it. It was too easy, but I guess someone on the Earthen plane wants me to win today. I'll take a win after all that's happened.

I open the door for Teari, close it, then go to the driver's side. It's an old Camry with plenty of legroom. Never thought I'd see myself driving an import. I close her door and survey the parking lot. I'm not sure what God looks like. Not sure this was left by him. I was told he's been gone for a long time... seems someone is offering guidance here. Probably eager to get me to leave.

After turning the ignition, I pull away from the hospital and head for the highway.

"What happened to your magical healing powers?" I ask.

"Too many blood transfusions. It will come back after a while." She holds up her hands. "I hope. The bones aren't done healing. Can't do much until I'm in tip top shape."

I guess that's what seems so different about her. She's lost some of her grace in the blood loss.

I fill her in on the shit show she missed while I abandoned her on the Earthen plane. I leave out a few details: Thrush, Nightingale's death, and my father being imprisoned. There will be time for that later.

"Sparrow's still a zombie," I say.

"Did he drink my blood?" Teari asks.

"He bit you. I'm not sure about the blood drinking part."

"My blood could heal him."

"Or not..." I warn.

"I can't give any now," she says. "What I have now is mostly donor. Billy-Bob Jenkins and Laura Doone don't have much in the way of angelic healing powers."

I nod. There's a tiny vial in my nightstand. I was saving it for something. Maybe this is it.

I drive to the Saratoga portal. The cemetery quite familiar now. The archway of the portal is demolished.

"Great," Teari says. "How will we get back now?"

"I'll take you," I say. "I just wanted to make sure it wasn't useable."

I take Teari's hand and *poof* we go to Hell together.

THIS IS HOW A HEART BREAKS

Teari's room is on the third floor. Just across the way from Jed and Shay and baby Thrush. Jed helped me with the runes on her door to keep her hidden. Later I'll talk to her about some tattoos, after she's had some time to heal.

After settling Teari into her new living space, I head to my room and grab the vial of her blood from the nightstand.

I make my way to the stairwell and jog down. Someone's coming up before I get very far.

I recognize the horns.

"What are you doing?" Skeele asks.

"Fixing him." I squeeze the vial in my palm before holding it up for him to see.

"Are you sure it's going to fix him?" Skeele rubs his chin. "It could do something... unexpected."

"Everything about this shit show is unexpected," I remind him, my eyes lingering on his mouth. I want to take him back to my room and finish what we started. "You're just pissed I left you in Vermont."

"I didn't need you to find my way back," he chuckles.

"Make the Hellion in the dungeon go away," I command.

Skeele nods. "As you wish."

I pause for a moment and let him get ahead of me. As I make my way to Sparrow's cell, the leaving Hellion passes me with a nod. I walk faster, eager to fix one of my problems.

"Open the door," I tell Skeele.

He walks in first and immobilizes Sparrow. I twist the cap off the vial of blood. Gripping Sparrow's upper arm to steady myself, I try not to focus on the fact that he's skin and bone now. Hallowed and sunken skin, he barely fights. His teeth snap together. I reach up on my tip toes and pour Teari's blood into his mouth.

Sparrow stops. He licks his lips. I shake the vial to get as much of the blood into his mouth as I can. When I'm done, a very small coating remains in the vial. I cap it and save it for later. I'm not below breaking the glass and licking the shards in an emergency.

Sparrow's head ticks to the side. A hand moves to his pocket and he pulls out a black feather.

"Sparrow?" I ask, desperation in my voice.

The milky coating clears, but something changes. Those aren't the Ireland-grass green eyes I remember. Were they ever green to begin with? He scans the surroundings, taking in the room, me, Skeele, the door. There's a sound forming deep in his throat.

Skeele lets go, grabs me, and drags me to the door. He slams it closed and locks it. Skeele holds my shoulder protectively.

"Where did he go?" Skeele asks.

"The only place he could go," I say. "He's been called back to his kingdom within the Seven Kingdoms of Heaven. With Nightingale dead, he takes the throne."

I didn't think it would happen so fast.

"What now?" Skeele asks, solemn and unimpressed.

Poof. I go to Nightingale's kingdom.

"Sparrow!" I call.

He's in the distance, inspecting the burned ruins of his home.

His curse finally cleared, he returns to nothing. Just ash and bone and sorrow.

One of the Archangels are there. It's not Gabriel. It's not his own father; I killed him a long time ago. One of the other Archangels who thinks this is my fault is standing close to Sparrow and telling him something.

"Sparrow?" I call. "Will you talk to me?"

He turns, focuses. There's my Sparrow. Finally. He runs toward me. I open my arms, running forward to leap in his arms like some cheesy romance movie. I don't care. He's back. My Sparrow is back. We get closer and closer. My heart fills with a joy I've never felt before. I've waited forever to feel like this, to have him free. To finally have set everything right.

"Sparrow," I say. "You're back. You're you."

"Is that so?" Sparrow asks. His voice is strange, not like I remember. There is no lilt of wonder and hope on his tongue. No Snowy Owl words. No moonlight whispers in the slick heat of lust. I do not recognize his voice at all.

He moves his arm and in the bright Heaven sun something glints in his hand. Sparrow is a trained Legion Commander and a Hellion leader. He knows how to fight the greatest of enemies. Teari's blood brought his strength back. He moves quicker than I've ever seen anything move. A quick jab. Three to my stomach. One to my thigh. Another to my arm. He holds the small blade against my breastbone and as I catch my breath, air thick with betrayal settles in my chest.

"An eye for an eye. Grace for grace," Sparrow's voice is malevolent, filled with hatred, like nothing I've ever heard. "Except you never had a speck of grace. I'll have to take something else."

He pushes the blade deeper until I feel the tip enter my heart.

Poof. I go back to Hell.

I collapse on the ground of the Hellions' lair. I didn't plan to drop at Skeele's feet, but I do.

"What in the hell happened?" is the last thing I hear.

-The End. Until next time. -

163

About the Author

M. R. Pritchard is a two-time Kindle Scout winning author, her short story GLITCH has been featured in the 2017 winter edition of THE FIRST LINE literary journal, and her short story MOON LORD has been featured in Chronicle Worlds: Half Way Home (Part of the Future Chronicles). M. R. Pritchard holds degrees in Biochemistry and Nursing. She is a northern New Yorker transplanted to the Gulf Coast of Florida who enjoys coffee, mint chocolate, cloudy days, and reading on the lanai.

Visit her website MRPritchard.com and sign up for her newsletter. You'll get a twice a month newsletter with updates, day to day shenanigans, and book deals.

Follow on Amazon to get alerts on new releases.

If you enjoyed *The Sparrow Man Series*, please leave a review, tell a friend, or gift to a friend. These small acts keep authors writing. Thank you.

ALSO BY M. R. PRITCHARD

<u>Science Fiction/post-apocalyptic:</u>

The Phoenix Project

The Reformation

Revelation

Inception

Origins

Resurrection

The Phoenix Project Compendium Edition

The Safest City on Earth

The Man Who Fell to Earth

Heartbeat

Asteroid Riders Series

Moon Lord

Collector of Space Junk and Rebellious Dreams

<u>Steampunk:</u>

Tick of a Clockwork Heart

<u>Dark Fantasy:</u>

Sparrow Man Series

Thread the Bone

NIGHTJAR

Skeele

"Christ," Skeele spit, followed by more swearing in Hellspeak as he bent to lift Meg from the ground. Not again, he thought. This can't be happening again. Skeele lifted Meg, one arm under her knees, another across her back.

The energy in the room went berserk. The new recruits were wild. Tukka and Chel did their best to calm them. But this was the kind of chaos that ensued when the throne was threatened. The throne was a coveted thing and could break an army. A shadowed realm where darkness reigns, the malevolence of the throne loomed, it had a presence. Lucifer's throne was steeped in sinister intentions, cunningly concealed beneath a shroud of deception woven by the very souls in subjugated. If Lucifer's rule was night, Meg's rule was day. She was a flicker of hope for the souls of Hell. She'd started to tame veil; she'd started to loosen the chains. The creatures of Hell required reigning in. For the first time in in eons, the Hellions were doing it with minimal violence.

Skeele lifted Meg, exhaling a breath of relief when he felt solid bones under her skin. It wasn't like last time. Last time he lifted her like this off the dusky grass of the back yard, it sounded like Rice Krispies crackling under her skin. He'd never heard nor felt the weight of someone with every bone in their body broken. Meg didn't remember and never understood his need to protect her ever since that day. She was hazardous to her own health ninety-nine percent of the time. Hellions didn't give a shit about much, but protecting their leader, they cared about that. He cared. He never wanted to experience lifting her as a bag of bones again. Yet, here he was.

"Get them out," Skeele shouted to Tukka and Chel as he walked toward the bar.

"I'll get the blood," Klaus shouted as he ran behind the bar, ripped open the fridge and tore out every bag of blood that was stocked there.

The energy of the room cooled as the other Hellions left.

Skeele dropped her lifeless body on the bar and slapped her face, trying to wake her. Blood leaked from wounds in her leg, arm, and stomach. The most concerning was the one over her heart. Gaping wide, he could see the slow pulse of her heart.

This wasn't medicine like on the Earthen place. Heaven and Hell had other methods of saving a life. Too bad Skeele wasn't skilled at any of them. None of the Hellions were. They needed something more, but battlefield survival would have to do.

Skeele and Tukka tore open the bags of blood and dripped them into Meg's mouth. The wounds seeped, their flow never seeming to stop.

Nothing happened. She didn't swallow. The blood simply pooled in her mouth. She was barely breathing and Skeele was so worked up he didn't believe his eyes to watch her shallow breaths.

"Pour it in the wounds," Tukka suggested.

"Can't hurt," Skeele said as he opened a fresh bag of blood and poured it over the stab wounds on her chest then her stomach.

Tukka ripped open another bag with his teeth and poured blood on her arm and leg wounds.

They waited. Nothing happened. Meg's breathing slowed. Her head tipped to the side with the pressure of his fingers as Tukka felt for a pulse, worry creasing his dark skin. He shook his head. "It's barely, anything. This is not good."

The blood in her mouth slowly dripped down her face. She looked dead. Worse than before. Worse than ever.

"I'm going to get help," Skeele said, running for the door.

Pre-order your copy of Nightjar on Kindle Now